THE YARD PEOPLE

DIANA BOTTONE

Edited by Helen Merritt
Interior and Cover Design by Woven Red Author Services
Stock imagery is acquired from Depositphotos Inc. via an on-demand contract.
Fonts are acquired through valid licences with various vendors.

The Yard People/Diana Bottone—1st edition, version 2
ISBN ebook: 979-8-9894760-1-5
ISBN paperback: 979-8-9894760-0-8

Acknowledgements

Alexandra DiBella - for inspiration.

Helen Merritt - for editing and encouragement.

Mary O'Neill - for putting me in contact
with Stanley B. Trice.

Stanley B. Trice - for the invaluable guidance.

Joan Frantschuk – for guidance and patience.

This book is dedicated to my father:
Antonio Joseph Bottone (Joe).

I promised him I would try to write a book
if he would purchase a computer
for me and my daughter.

I wish I had completed it before
his death in 1998.

Author's Note

Most of this story takes place in the mid 1990s. It's set in Eastern North Carolina, in a town called New Bern, at a time just before technology was peaking. Cell phones were very new, so not many people had them. There was no social media, and no readily access to the internet. Desktop computers were in the workplace and in some homes. Music was still purchased in stores on Compact Discs (CD's) and cassette tapes, with grunge rock and rap being popular. Most people had cable TV, with sitcoms and police dramas being popular. There were video stores where movies could be rented on VHS tapes to be played and watched on a VCR in the home. Smoking cigarettes was still regarded as an acceptable vice and was permitted in most places.

I wrote this story after observing some neighbors, and they sparked my imagination. This story is fictional, and in no way represents any real people. Any similarities to persons in New Bern, or anywhere else, is purely coincidental. I wrote this story in the mid 1990s, however I didn't tweak it for publishing until almost 28 years later.

1

Ten Years Earlier

There was no excuse. The night was clear and the moon was bright. The James family was on their way home from spending 4th of July weekend at their beach cottage on Emerald Isle. Dr. Clayton James had the stereo jamming out on the rock station. The loud rock music was getting on the nerves of his wife, Leanne James. Fifteen-year-old Mark James was in the back seat entertaining his adored little brother, six-year-old Kevin James. Rather than ask Clayton to turn down the volume, Leanne abruptly reached over and turned off the car stereo. Clayton started to protest, but seeing the set jaw on his wife's face, he thought better of it. The two-lane highway leading away from the beach is a long, straight stretch. Clayton, having been beaten by sun, wind and alcohol for most of the long weekend, was starting to cave from exhaustion, and with the exaggerated quiet and the hypnotizing highway his mind, which had a tendency to be weak, was beginning to drift into the "no-zone".

Dr. Clayton James had never viewed the recovery room at County Regional Hospital from a prone position. It took him several minutes to adjust to his whereabouts. It took him much longer to adjust to the news he had received. Leanne James: dead. Mark James: broken neck and back. Kevin James: bruised, but relatively unharmed. As for himself: Concussion, broken left leg, and the beginnings of a tortured soul.

2

Present Day

Although Amy had mixed feelings about moving into the new house, well, only new to them, her mother Linda was over the moon about it. The little house was rather old, it was built in the 1940's. It was located in one of the older neighborhoods of their small quaint town of New Bern, NC. Amy was excited about the two of them being out on their own, but she was a little nervous about leaving the security of her grandparent's home. They had lived with her grandparents since her mom left her dad three years earlier. This new house was in what Amy considered to be a mediocre neighborhood, but it might be fun. Some of her friends from school lived nearby and she would be able to walk to school with them since the middle school was just down the street. She could skate or ride her bike here too and there was a park nearby. Linda loved older neighborhoods because of the abundance of mature trees and shrubbery. To her the newer neighborhoods looked so baren.

"These old homes have great bones." the Realtor assured Linda Sabre at the closing. Linda didn't require much convincing though. She was elated to finally be independent.

Living with Mom and Dad was comfortable, and it was a huge help to her financially, but she always had that sense of failure. Now she was back on her feet and feeling great. Not that she had hit the big time. She knew it was going to be somewhat of a struggle, perhaps living from paycheck to paycheck at times, but she was in charge of her life again.

The new house was a quaint two-bedroom bungalow. It had a big shaded front porch, which was important to Linda - she had always considered herself a porch monkey. There were hard-wood floors throughout, and an eat-in kitchen. The doorways from the living room to the kitchen and from the living room to the hallway were arched, which really added character. The backyard was fenced and there was a big tree in the center of the yard, the kind of tree kids love to climb. It would provide lovely shade in the summer and an array of beautiful colors in the fall. Linda was already imagining a picnic table and grill back there. The neighboring houses were close, but not "in your face" close. This place would be just fine.

The following week Amy was flopped out on the couch. She was worn out from moving boxes and clothes all day. All the furniture and things were finally inside. Some of Linda's friends from her job had helped them move. Afterwards, Linda provided them pizza and beer, but now they had all gone home. Linda was sitting on the floor just staring into space, basking in a moment of relaxation.

"Mom," Amy said, "I hope the neighbors are cool."

"What, Baby?" Linda looked up at her.

"You know, the neighbors. I hope they're not weird. My friend Megan has a neighbor that always hangs out in his front yard watering the grass all day. She says he always has some stupid comment to say to anybody that walks by. She says she tries to walk on the other side of the street so he won't start talking to her."

"What kind of stupid comments does he say, Amy?"

"Well, Megan says he'll say stuff like, 'Don't you think your shirt's getting a little tight?' and stuff like that."

"Damn, he sounds like a pervert. I hope she tells her parents what he says. Anyway, all neighborhoods have weirdos like that, usually just one. Don't worry. But be nice, Amy, not all people are perfect like us!" Linda laughed. "Strange folks do make life interesting. Let's go get some ice cream & chips."

By ten-o-clock their tummies were filled with junk food and they were exhausted. Too tired to find their bed linens, Amy chose to sleep on the living room couch and Linda crashed out on her bare mattress with a light blanket. It was unusually cool for late August in Eastern North Carolina. They slept deep with the windows open. Even the loud cicadas didn't disturb their slumber. But by seven the next morning Linda felt as though she had only slept ten minutes. She was scrambling around the house trying to pull herself together for work. *God, I wish we could have moved in on Saturday instead of Sunday!* she was thinking. *What I wouldn't give for an extra day to settle in and rest.* Amy was still sleeping on the couch when Linda rushed out the door with her keys. While pulling out of the driveway, she noticed a junked up looking pickup truck parked in front of the house next door with some people sitting in it. *Didn't I see that same truck parked there last night when we came in from our junk food run?* she thought. *I hate people seeing me leave for work. I might as well be hailing a neon sign saying "I'm leaving now... Won't be back for eight hours... Go ahead and rob my house!" Damn, I sound like a paranoid bitch.*

It was close to ten thirty when Amy was awakened by the phone. "Hey sleepyhead." said Linda. "Go ahead and start unpacking things and putting them where they belong. Except for the kitchen stuff - I have my ways, you know."

"Okay Mom. What about lunch?"

"I'll be there around twelve fifteen with something. I love you, bye."

I love me some fast food, but we need some real food up in here, Amy was thinking. The first things Amy unpacked was the stereo, CD's and cassette tapes. She was rocking out pretty good to some Pearl Jam and making some headway with her bedroom when she heard a loud motor outside. She went out on the porch and saw an older model car parked in front of the house next door. There were people in it - an old woman, an old man and a boy that looked about her age, thirteen, maybe fourteen. The old man and woman looked like what she thought of as "hill people". She didn't know why she thought that - she had never lived in the hills. Maybe it was something she had seen on television once. They were dressed poorly and the woman had long, stringy gray hair pulled back in a head band. Then the people who lived in the house came out to talk to them. The man was large and lumbering and his son, who looked about sixteen was the same way. *They don't look right,* she thought and went back inside. Soon after that she heard the car pull away. By the time her mom came home with lunch, Amy had her bedroom and the bathroom pretty much put together.

"Mom, when can you get my computer all connected?" Amy asked. "There's no cable for the TV yet, and I'm sooooo bored." Amy's grandfather had recently bought a desktop computer for her. It had Solitaire and Mahjong games on it that she wanted to play.

"When have you had time to get bored?" Besides the cable should be connected before I get home from work this evening. I have to get some groceries on the way home, so I'll be about forty-five minutes late. If I have the energy, I'll hook your computer up tonight. It won't take long, but I have so many other things that need to be taken care of. Especially this kitchen!"

"I can do the kitchen. I kind of remember how you had the kitchen before the big d-i-v-o-r-c-e." Amy liked to sing-spell out the word divorce like the Tammy Wynette song. "Trust me." she said with a devilish side glance as she tapped her fingers together. Linda always delighted in Amy's sense of humor.

"Oh, alrighty then, Amy. You do the kitchen and I'll put your computer on 'top priority'. Gotta go now. I love you." Linda had experience hooking up computers to monitors, keyboards, and printers from doing it at work, and she was already on her way out the door to go back.

3

Linda worked as a secretary/assistant for a building contractor. She was very adept with computer programs, maps and blueprints. She liked her job and it kept her in contact with a lot of interesting people. She was a perfectionist at work, quite in contrast to her personal life. Her boss, Michael, had come to depend on her tremendously. The only downside to her job was the envy it produced in her. Every day she saw plans for beautiful homes built for people who, in her mind, were no smarter than her, and most of the time not as smart. *Why did they deserve such lovely homes when I have to struggle just to live in a small, unassuming house?* She tried to not think this way, but sometimes it just couldn't be helped. She knew she was living in a time when two incomes were imperative for success, coupled with a college degree, both of which she was lacking.

"Linda, I need you to get a building permit for the Carlton job this afternoon." Michael called from his office in the back.

Aw shit! Linda thought. *The last thing I wanted today was to have to deal with that dragon lady at Building Inspections.* "I'm on it," she called back cheerfully.

Walking into the Building Inspections office was always unpleasant. The dragon lady, or 'Bitchy Niki' as she was referred to by most, sat at the desk typing, or pretending to, never looking up. *I know she heard me come in.* "Good afternoon." Linda said. Niki looked up and just stared at Linda with a dead look in her eyes. *She must live a miserable life.* Linda thought. Niki was a young, very attractive woman with a major attitude. She acted like she hated the world and everyone in it. It appeared the only thing she cared about was her hair, nails and clothing accessories. She was always changing her hair with different colors and hair pieces, and she had these long claw-like fingernails that must be glued on. *Bacteria breeders!* She wore a vulgar amount of jewelry and her shoes always matched her clothes. Her makeup was flawless at all times. Niki was the epitome of 'high maintenance' and 'self-indulgence'.

"I need a permit for this job." Linda said as she offered the paperwork. "Here are all the necessary papers."

Niki slowly looked through all the paperwork, with a look on her face like the papers had an odor, and then finally said, "You have to pay $300 today and the permit will be ready in one week. Do you want to pick it up?"

"Yes, I'll pick it up. Will you call me when it's ready? Linda asked.

"Just call this office in one week to see if it's ready." Niki replied as she resumed typing.

Linda wrote the check, handed it over, and waited for the receipt. No more words were spoken between the two. *She's got everyone by the balls.* Linda was thinking. *If anyone was to comment or complain about her attitude, she could hold up a permit for months. I'll be damned if I'm going to compliment her over-accessorized outfit the way the folks at Jim's Custom Builders do just to make her treat me like a human being. Nope, I'm not kissing her ass.* Linda knew of one contractor who gave Nicki a turkey every

Thanksgiving so that his permits didn't get held up. *I hope Michael never starts doing that.*

Linda picked up some Andy's Carolina cheeseburgers - with mustard, chili & coleslaw, after grocery shopping. She knew she and Amy were overdoing the fast food, but what the hell. She wasn't going to feel like cooking by the time she finished putting groceries away and setting up the computer. Amy was eagerly waiting for her mom when Linda arrived. The junky pickup was once again parked in front of the house next door, again with people just sitting in it.

"Those people never get out of their cars, Mom." Amy said excitedly.

"What are you talking about?" Linda asked.

"Next door. Whenever someone comes to visit them, they never go in the house. They just sit in their cars and the people come out and stand in the yard and talk to them. Or no one comes out, and the people visiting just sit in their car! Isn't that weird?"

"Isn't it weird that you're watching them so much? Are you a 'Peeping Amy'? Linda started laughing. Although, in her mind she kind of felt the same way. But it was just their first full day in this neighborhood and maybe something was happening with the next-door neighbors on this particular day. "I doubt this is a daily ritual, Amy. Maybe those people ran an ad to sell something, and people are coming by to inquire. No one lets strangers in their homes now-a-days. Let's put these groceries up and eat, then I'll tackle the computer. I wouldn't mind playing some games on it myself. Mahjong relaxes me."

4

The first week in their new house went by quickly and uneventful. The cool spell ended and the air conditioning was working great. Summer certainly wasn't over yet. Amy was all set to start school soon but Linda was in the mood for a party at her new place. This weekend would be great – Labor Day Weekend. Three glorious days off! Linda's best friend Karen, who was the drafts-person at work, was more than willing to help pull off a cookout with all the fixings, and beer was her favorite fixing.

Karen had an unusual beauty. She was about five-foot ten inches, with skin that always looked slightly tanned. Her long thick hair was a medium ash brown and her eyes were a pale gray with the longest, darkest eyelashes that are usually reserved for men. She was twenty-eight, ten years younger than Linda, and she was very intelligent and a lot of fun. Linda thought the world of her. Most women didn't like to be seen with Karen because of her beauty, and every now and then it would get to Linda somewhat as well because Linda, although attractive, was barely five-foot two inches. She had long dark brown hair, which was straight and silky, and she had smallish but pretty dark brown eyes that revealed her emotions.

Linda, Amy and Karen had spent most of that Saturday on the strand at the Atlantic Beach. They body surfed for a while, then bobbed in the calmer, deeper waters and spotted some dolphins. Amy later collected seashells while her mom & Karen worked on their suntans. After they got home and were all showered & refreshed, Amy went to her grandparents' house for the night.

Linda and Karen and about twelve more of their friends, mostly subcontractors and plumbers and their dates or spouses, partied into the night in Linda's back yard. Karen's boyfriend Richard brought his grill and everyone brought their own chairs. Linda made sure the music wasn't too loud, but by about eleven PM they decided to move the party inside anyway. At some point during the night, Richard decided to answer nature's call in the back yard, the way men love to do to reaffirm their freedom. When he came back in it was through the front door.

"Hey, your neighbors are standing out in their front yard talking to some folks in a car. I hope they're not planning to call the law." Richard said. "You really can't hear the music from out there though."

Linda didn't know why, but she started feeling uncomfortable after hearing that. *The neighbors aren't doing anything out of the ordinary, Linda. Stop feeling creepy!* She thought. She continued to have a good time, hell-bent on having a hangover, although somewhere in the back of her mind she couldn't shake the feeling that something was amiss next door.

The party broke up around two-thirty AM – this crowd had stamina. Karen spent the night on the couch. Linda woke up around nine-thirty the next morning and got into the shower. The hot water felt so good to her pounding head. *I Should've taken a BC powder before getting in the shower.* Karen was still asleep when Linda began picking up cans and bottles and emptying ash trays. Once that was done, the place really didn't look too bad, although it could use some airing out.

Looking at Karen, Linda thought *How can she just sleep like that? It must be because she's not a mom. I recall when I used to could sleep through anything, but that was before I had Amy. Wow, I haven't been in a real dead sleep for over thirteen years!* "Hey! Karen! Wake up! Let's pick up Amy and go to Billy's to get some breakfast."

Karen opened one eye and looked at Linda with it. After a hazy moment she sat up and stretched. "Where's Richard?"

Linda hadn't even thought about Richard. They looked in Amy's room and there he was asleep on the floor. He was just beginning to stir.

5

Linda, Amy, Karen and Richard sat in a booth at Billy's, the local twenty-four-hour diner, drinking coffee and Diet Coke and waiting on their food. Linda had a cast-iron stomach along with a healthy appetite, and she was having the spicy Spanish Omelet with a side of grits. Amy and Richard both opted for pancakes and sausage. Karen was getting a little nauseous from the smell of sausage and other fried horrors (her words). She had a delicate stomach for a young woman, and she was borderline vegetarian. She was having waffles with fruit.

"We need to get you a man, Linda." Karen announced out of the blue.

Linda looked up from her chili-smothered omelet and replied sarcastically "Why? I've had a man before. Several actually."

"Yeah" Amy said rolling her eyes. "And we don't want any more of them around, do we Mom?" Linda just cut Amy a look which was interpreted as "'Enough of that."

Amy then continued to eat her pancakes, getting some of her long, blonde hair sticky with syrup. Amy had her mother's olive complexion, but was quite a contrast with the blond hair and bright blue eyes. Her eyes had been described by some as being the shade of faded blue jeans. Linda always said they looked like blue crystals. Amy was a very pretty girl and already taller than her mother. She was getting her height from her grandma. Linda got her short stature from Amy's Grampa.

Richard said, "I know a guy. He's kind of arrogant, but he's alright. He's a little old, probably forty something and divorced, but I could fix you up."

"Yes!" Karen exclaimed excitedly. "We could all go out together, have dinner, go dancing, or whatever – it would be fun!"

"Mom..." Amy drug the word out to three syllables and got this pleading look on her face.

Amy doesn't like to share. Linda was thinking. *But it's been a while since I've been on a date and I'm not getting any younger.* "Maybe." Linda said, ignoring Amy's plea. "But it would definitely have to be a double date with you two. I'm not going out with a 'strange man' unescorted." she said with a devilish grin on her face. And laughing she said "Someone has to protect him!" Linda thought she was so clever sometimes. Amy was looking embarrassed at this point.

6

By Monday evening, the end of the three-day Labor Day Weekend, Linda and Amy had their home in order with time to rest. Linda was in her rocker on the porch enjoying the warm summer evening air. Warm summer evenings were one of the simple things that made her feel so good. Tomorrow she would start her week refreshed and Amy would begin the eighth grade. As she gently rocked, sipping occasionally on a glass of wine, her mind drifted. She was drifting back to when she left Amy's father three years earlier. He had turned out to be a very irresponsible husband and father, and when Linda lost respect for him, there was no turning back. She hated to disrupt her daughter's life at such a vulnerable age, but Amy was strong. She adapted well to them living at her grandparent's. It helped that they loved her so and enjoyed spoiling her. Now Amy would have to adapt again. It wouldn't be hard. *Hell, my parents are only two miles away.* Linda loved her parents dearly. *If only they acted like they loved each other! They hardly tolerate each other. They had been married more than forty years; they should have mellowed by now.*

Linda's mom Sharon was such a free spirit. She seemed to have a sixth sense about her too, like she could sense things about people in an uncanny way. Also, if you displeased her, she certainly let you know. But she was a very protective mom. Her dad Jim was a retired Marine and he had a lot of integrity. He did his best in everything he attempted. He was short in stature, but he never had 'short man syndrome'. He was always a gentleman and had unconditional love for Linda and Amy. When Linda and Amy moved in with them, Linda never dreamed it would be for three years. But now she's on her own front porch relaxing. Life is good.

Linda was so caught up in her thoughts that she almost didn't notice the man next door walking around by his front stoop. When she did focus on him, she noticed that he seemed to be moving around somewhat aimlessly. This was her first good look at him. He was a tall, large man with white curly hair. It was too dark to make out any facial features, but she started feeling uncomfortable (why?) and she went into her house.

7

"I don't ever want to have sex." Amy said out of the blue one brisk October afternoon.

"Good!" Linda replied. "But what brought this on?"

"Well," Amy paused. "I have something to tell you, Mom. Don't get mad, okay?"

Linda wasn't sure how to respond. She couldn't very well promise not to get mad, but she wanted Amy to open up to her. "You know you can talk to me, Baby."

Averting her eyes, Amy began, "This morning Megan wanted me to come to her house a little early before walking to school. Her mom was already at work and Megan showed me this video tape. It was disgusting!"

Linda put her hands up palms out, as if to stop Amy. "Did she show you a porn movie?!"

Linda was so relieved that it wasn't anything more serious, but she couldn't reveal her relief. "I can't believe she did that. I have heard Megan is a little wild for her age, but damn. Where did she get it?"

"I think it belongs to her mom."

Linda was trying not to laugh. *The nut doesn't fall too far from the tree.* "Sex is pretty gross, isn't it? I'm sorry you had to see that. But I do want you to understand that those kinds of movies just show pure raw sex with no emotion or feelings.

It's really not that way when two adults are in love and really care for each other, plus they usually do it in the dark. Anyway, at your age I'm glad you're turned off by it. I'm not going to pick your friends for you, but I don't want you going to Megan's when her mom's not there anymore. I'm sure her mother wouldn't appreciate her entertaining friends in the house when she's gone, dirty movies or not."

Linda didn't much care for Megan's mom, and this situation really came as no surprise. Megan's mom Connie was well-known in high school for all the wrong reasons. She was openly promiscuous, but worse than that she was a bully. She was very pretty, with her raven black hair, green eyes and curvy figure, but she made fun of girls who weren't so attractive. She just had a mean streak in her and Linda never understood why.

"Are you going to tell her mom?"

No. I don't know Connie that well (*not really true*) and I don't want to embarrass her. I never would've figured her to have dirty movies though (*again not true, she probably has a full library of them*) and I don't want her to know that I know. Amy, I'm glad you talked to me about this, and I'm sorry it happened."

Kids these days. And that Megan looks so innocent for the wild child she is. Amy was old enough to be home by herself for a few hours after school before Linda got home from work. Linda hoped she was doing the right thing by trusting Amy to make the right decisions, especially with a friend like Megan. But Linda remembered having had many a friend like Megan when she was growing up and she managed to use common sense and stay out of trouble. *At least I never got caught when I made bad choices.*

Fortunately, Amy was enjoying eighth grade and excelling in her classes. They both had adjusted very well to their new home.

8

Seven Years Earlier

The first few years after the accident Dr. Clayton James still seemed to be in shock. He tried to keep up his medical practice. He had hired a full-time nurse to care for Mark, who was paralyzed from the neck down. Mark had also lost his ability to speak or take food orally. All he really had left was the ability to comprehend. The nurse also looked after Kevin when he wasn't in school.

Dr. James didn't grieve much over the death of his wife. They started out so happy together. But over the years she became more and more materialistic and very critical of others, especially of him. He also wanted to blame her for the horrible accident that evening, but he knew it was all on him. He had literally snuffed out any kind of life Mark could have ever had. Dr. James agonized over that. Mark had such potential! And then there was Kevin. Growing up without a mother. And the brother he had idolized so very much was unable to even talk to him. Poor, wasted Mark. All he had was his mind. And his mind was slowly wasting due to severe lack of stimulation.

Being so full of remorse and guilt, Dr. James' practice suffered. He no longer had the presence of mind to feel confident in surgery, and finally he had no choice but to retire from the medical field. Then the money started running out... Then the nurse had to be let go... Then they had to downsize...

9

Present Day

It was Saturday night. Linda was shivering with anticipation. She hadn't been on a date in ages. Karen and Richard had finally arranged a double date and tonight was the night. Amy was glad to go stay at her grandparents'; she was missing them. Linda was almost overcome with anxiety as she tried to apply her lipstick. She hoped her floral print mini dress paired with a jean jacket and flat pumps wasn't too casual. *Are you this nervous because you're horny? Calm down. You know what most men are all about – you got this.* She was annoyed with herself for feeling so adolescent. She heard the car pull up then heard the door shut closed. *This is it. Pull yourself together.* She opened the front door to come face-to-face with a very conservative looking man in his mid-forty's. *This isn't anyone I'd give a second glance to in a grocery store.* Immediately her nerves began to calm.

"Hi, I'm George Matthews," he spoke. George was a full six-feet tall with broad shoulders. He had a filled-out, manly build, exaggerated by the way he was puffing himself out with his thumbs tucked in his front pants pockets. He was wearing khaki pants and a white button-down shirt with the long sleeves buttoned at the cuffs. He wore glasses and his light brown hair was sparse on top. His sideburns were short and his full (non-chiseled) face was clean-shaven. He was fair complected – very Anglo looking.

"Come in, George." Linda said with a big smile. "Can I get you a beer?"

"No thanks. You're a pretty little thing, aren't you?" He spoke slow and deliberately.

Oh, God. Linda was eye-rolling in her mind. "Thank you. Where are we meeting Karen and Richard?"

On the way to the restaurant Linda was sizing up George. *He _is_ arrogant. It's not so much what says, it's how he says it and how he carries himself.* Most of the conversation was about him. What he does, what his interests are (*himself*) and so on. And that gun on the car seat! She wasn't used to being close to a gun. Linda was trying to not regret the evening before it started. After all, she too was somewhat arrogant and so she decided to give him a chance. Maybe he was nervous too.

Karen and Richard picked their favorite local restaurant, Annabelle's. It was comfortable-casual with a touch of elegance. They were already seated when Linda and George arrived. Their presence made Linda feel at ease. Richard cleaned up nicely. Usually, a tee shirt and jeans man, he was wearing nice navy slacks with a long-sleeved polo shirt. Richard is a free-lance photographer and does quite well at it. He and Karen met when he was shooting some of Michael's homes for a local magazine. Of course, he just *had* to photograph her, and the rest is history. Karen looked drop-dead gorgeous in a strappy black dress and sandals. Turns out George is a people person. He enjoyed entertaining the group with funny stories, and he was a gentleman, meaning he didn't mind spending his money on Linda. The more she observed him, the more endearing he became (*or was that the wine?*). Linda felt he had a sweetness to him that he wasn't comfortable showing – he seemed guarded in way she couldn't pinpoint. However, she was becoming more infatuated with him as the evening progressed, and she was pretty sure it wasn't the wine.

Linda learned George owned a sporting goods store in Havelock. Havelock is a small military town located between New Bern and the coast. George's sporting goods store catered mainly to hunters and weight-lifters, not athletes. He carried guns of all kinds, small boats, kayaks and canoes, tents and that sort of thing. He also carried free weights and benches and had an area in the store for clients to work out, and he had a shooting range in the back. Linda wasn't real crazy about the name of his establishment: A Man's World. She really was hoping he had more late-twentieth century ideals. George himself was into weight-lifting, and, she learned, he goes nowhere without his gun.

"It's crazy for a man to be without a gun." he said. "You can stop any problem that comes up if you have your gun."

This was the only thing so far that Linda was really uneasy about. She thought he sounded paranoid. But he did seem responsible enough, he was forty-five years old, owned his own business, and had never been arrested for anything. *That's right Linda. Keep justifying his weirdness. You've been alone too long, I guess.*

It was late when they arrived home. Linda invited George inside and opened two beers. She noticed he only had one drink at the restaurant, which was refreshing to see in a man. Still, she wanted a beer and didn't want to drink alone. She put on some music, this was probably not the thing to do on a first date, and sat with him on the couch. Before she knew it he was kissing her gently. He knew just how to do it and she was feeling herself let go. Then he began pressing and she could hear and feel his breathing and it caused such a rush insider her that she became the aggressor. So many forgotten sensations were coming alive within her that she thought she would explode. *To hell with first date rituals...* she was thinking as they passionately made their way to her bed.

10

"So, what'd you think of George?" Karen asked over the phone the next morning.

"He's different. Question is... 'what does he think of me?'" Linda replied.

"I'm sure he -" then Karen picked up on Linda's tone. "Did you do the dirty last night, little mommy?"

Big sigh over the phone. "Yes, Ma'am. And it was just what I needed... and more than I could have imagined! But now, of course I feel guilty and he probably won't ask me out again."

"You still live in the Dark Ages, Linda. You're both adults, not to worry! If you were any *good,* he'll ask you out again, I'm sure."

"Oh, God. It's not just a measure of morality anymore, now it's a measure of performance too? If that's the case, I think he'll call." Linda laughed. "But if he doesn't, where can I get lessons?" Talking with Karen eased Linda's guilt. But guilt or no guilt, she couldn't get the stupid grin off her face. If he never called it would be a night worth remembering. *Who knew I could be so aggressive?!* She was feeling younger and more alive than she had for some time.

After saying goodbye to Karen, Linda got up to let some light in the house. When she opened the blinds, she noticed the old car parked in front of the neighbor's house with people sitting in it. *Don't they even know anyone with newer cars?* She wondered. She brushed it off and went to take a shower. She knew she could relive last night one more time while in the hot, steamy shower.

11

Monday morning when Linda got to work, she spoke briefly with the receptionist Cindy, and then went directly to Karen's office. "I saw the strangest thing yesterday. You know those religious guys that ride bikes and go from house to house to spread the word? Mormons, I believe? Anyway, I wouldn't answer the door when they came, but when they left, I watched through the window. They went over to the Yard People's house."

"The Yard People?" Karen interrupted.

"Oh yeah, that's what Amy nicknamed those people, you know, I told you about them. Their visitors never leave their cars, never go inside the house. And the people that live there just stand in the yard to talk with them."

"Oh, right." Karen made a frowny face. "Go ahead."

"Well, this was the first time I've *ever* seen anyone go inside their house since I've lived there. But what's weird is when those guys came back out. They seemed, I don't know, lost? They started slowly walking down the street, and get this, they completely forgot about their bikes! Then, the boy that lives there came out and hollered 'Get your bikes!'. So, they looked at each other, and came back and got on their bikes and left. But then they went the *opposite* way from the direction they were *just* walking!"

"Do you think the yard people got them high?" Karen was serious.

Linda just broke out in laughter. Almost uncontrollable laughter. "Oh Karen! You always bring me back to Earth!" Then, regaining her composure, "I think maybe I've seen too many movies, but you have to admit, it is strange."

"Why don't you go over there one day and introduce yourself? Meet these 'yard people' and quit spooking yourself."

"Yeah, *that'll* happen." Linda replied jokingly. "Talk about spooking myself, I have to go to Building Inspections today. Want to go with me? Maybe Bitchy Niki's fingernails are clashing with her lipstick, or maybe her belt's a different color from her shoes. Nah, never happen. I'd like to know whose dick she's licking to keep that job."

"Linda! That's vulgar, even for you."

"I know."

Later that morning Linda walked into the Inspections office expecting the usual rude indifference. To her surprise, Chief Building Inspector Manning was sitting in the front office with Niki (very unusual). Niki looked up and smiled. "Hi. Can I help you?"

Linda was speechless for a moment. "Um, hi Niki. Hello Chief Manning, it's a pleasure to run in to you."

"Howdy Linda" the Chief replied pleasantly. "You tell Michael he's been runnin' my ass around all over this county. He needs to slow down building them houses." Niki giggled girlishly at his remarks.

"I'll tell him, but I'm here with more plans and we're ready for the finals on the Carlton job."

"Alright then. You take it easy, girl." he said with a smile and went upstairs to his office.

Niki was just staring at Linda now, no more smile, and they went through their usual routine. *So that's how it is.* Linda realized. *Niki's a charmer when the boss is around and a real shit otherwise.*

Linda was back at her desk finalizing a contract when the phone rang. Cindy was off on an errand, so Linda picked up. "Michael Angelo Homes" she answered. Some didn't believe it, but Michael Angelo is Michael's real name. So, he capitalized on the artist Michelangelo's name. His slogan read: *Michael Angelo Homes; Live in a Work of Art.* Linda thought it was sounded kind of cheesy, but he did build beautiful homes. He didn't even need a salesperson on his team, his homes sold themselves, along with word-of-mouth from very satisfied clients.

"This is George Matthews. I'd like to speak to Linda please." George thought he recognized her voice, but he wanted to be sure.

Just a flash of judgment crossed Linda's mind. *Speak to? Not speak with?* "Hi George. This is Linda"

"If you don't already have plans, would you like to go out to dinner with me Friday night?"

"That would be nice." Her heart going thump, thump, thump. "What time should I expect you?"

"I'll pick you up at 7:30. Bye." And he hung up.

"Karen!' Linda called across the hall. "He called! I have a date with George Friday night!"

"I told you! You had nothing to worry about. Where are you two going?" Karen replied excitedly.

"I have no idea." Linda was laughing. "He sure isn't very chatty on the phone. But that's kind of nice."

They didn't realize Michael had come in. "I didn't realize I had high school girls working for me. What's all the excitement?" He inquired.

"Linda's getting a life." Karen replied dryly.

12

Five Years Earlier

Mark James was becoming resentful, perhaps revengeful. He had lived a short, fulfilled life then had it snatched away in an instant. For the past two years he saw the same walls, the same ceiling, the same morbid, weak father, the same sad-eyed brother. Ever since they moved him into this small room, he no longer received physical therapy and no one was reading to him. They provided no television, was there even one in the house? He missed the attention he used to get from the nurse. All that was becoming a fading memory. He had no idea where he now lived, if you could call it living. He no longer resented his family for his *physical* condition. Now, it was his *mind*. He was losing his mind, and he *hated* them for it.

His family did nothing to stimulate or engage him. They only felt pity for him, therefore they avoided him, and the isolation was crippling his mind. What memories he had were fast fading, and there had been no new ones to replace them. Why wouldn't they just talk to him? Tell him about their day, or play music or make up stories? Were they afraid he would become jealous? Anything would be better than nothing at all.

Mark had to do something – for he did not know how to die. He had to probe deep within his mind and learn how to reach out for some kind of relief, some kind of escape. *New memories!* He needed new memories to keep him going. At least now he knew what he needed and it gave him something to concentrate on. This would be his project. He had given himself something to strive for, if he could make it work.

13

Present Day

Amy wasn't thrilled to learn her mother had another date with this man George, and she didn't want to spend the night away this time. Linda agreed to let her stay home. After all, she was old enough. Linda knew Amy missed her father, although he made little attempt to contact her since the divorce. Amy was nine when Linda and he separated, and Amy still thinks he walks on water. Seeing Linda with another man is very awkward for her.

Linda was concerned about the fact she had already slept with George, and she really didn't know him or know much about him. She wasn't sure how to go about getting to know him. She didn't want to come across as clingy or nosy. Linda wasn't actually looking for a relationship, but a one-night stand wasn't for her either. *Just enjoy the evening.* She told herself. *With Amy home it's not likely you'll get laid tonight anyway, then see if he bothers calling again. That should tell you something.*

George took Linda to Federal Allely, a nice restaurant in the downtown section of their small city. Downtown New Bern is an historical district. New Bern is the second oldest city in North Carolina and was the State Capital in Colonial times. The locals take a great deal of pride in this, so much so that the Historical Preservation Committee is jokingly referred to as the Hysterical Committee. It's a beautiful town nestled at the convergence of two rivers, and it attracts a lot of tourism. It was a romantic setting for a date.

George seemed to take much care in making Linda feel like a lady. He was very attentive and generous. But he is human and he did tease her somewhat about how wild she had been in bed last weekend. He got her to blush a few times until she'd had enough.

"Would you have preferred me to have been less excited? Bored with you perhaps?" She quipped.

His eyes got big. "No ma'am." He replied earnestly. "You were all the woman I could handle, and I loved it. I'll behave now." He slightly bowed his head and lost some of his arrogance. "I'm sorry I over-stepped."

Linda had a sense George was a little excited when he answered her, although his body language said otherwise. *Odd*, she thought.

They moved on to other conversations. She told him about her job with Michael Angelo Homes. She has been with Michael for the past eight years now. She calls herself a glorified secretary because she still does all the secretarial work, but she's really Michael's right arm and he pays her pretty well for it. She has conferences with prospective clients, does all the paperwork and leg work for obtaining permits, meets with planners, and so on. She declined to mention that she and Michael were an item at one time. But that was way before she worked for him. It was before she met and married Amy's father. *Michael was the one that got away*, her mind drifted a bit.

George said he was divorced going on five years now. He didn't volunteer anything about his ex-wife, which was fine with Linda. He has a daughter, Liz who is twenty-three and lives in Raleigh. She stayed there after graduating from NC

State, and works with the State Department of Energy. And he has a son Jake, not short for Jacob, who is twenty-one and serving in the Army – not by choice. It was that or do a stint in prison for petty larceny.

Then he went on about hunting and some other interests he has. George liked to talk... a lot. He had a smooth, soothing voice however. Linda found comfort in his voice even if what he was saying didn't always interest her.

After dinner they enjoyed a leisurely stroll around Union Point Park. The air coming off the river was brisk and refreshing, and the fallen dried leaves made lovely crispy sounds as they danced in the breeze. Linda loved Autumn in New Bern,

"Would you like to come in and meet Amy?" Linda asked as George was walking her to her door. It was around eleven-thirty. "I'm sure she's still up."

"Yeah okay." George replied non-enthusiastically.

"To be honest, George, she's just as thrilled about you as you are about her." Linda said with a laugh. "We don't have to do this now."

"It's fine." George replied. "Rip the band-aid."

Amy was lounging on the couch with a cola watching a movie. "Hey Mom" she said as Linda and George were coming through the door.

"Hey sweetie" Linda replied with a smile. "This is George Matthews. George this is Amy."

"Aren't little girls supposed to be in bed at this hour?" George said to Amy before Amy had a chance to say anything. He had a stupid grin on his face.

"Nice meeting you too." Amy replied sarcastically, and got up to go to her room.

George started laughing. "Look at her, she's mad. You don't have to go to bed, I'm teasing you. I'm leaving anyway."

Lordy this isn't going well at all, thought Linda.

George was still chuckling when he kissed Linda lightly on the cheek. "Good night girls. I had a nice time, Linda." And he was out the door.

"What do you see in him?" Amy demanded.

"I'm not sure yet, but I enjoy his company. Or maybe I've just been lonely and didn't realize it? He likes to tease for sure, I found that out earlier. I know it can be annoying, but try to find your sense of humor when he's here, okay? That's if he comes back." Linda hated that she had become so insecure, she was so confident in her younger days.

14

Amy and Megan were walking around the neighborhood after school one cool autumn day, like they usually did, critiquing cars as they went. The more expensive the better. Of course, they both agreed on that. Amy mostly liked the bigger type cars, like a Cadillac or a Lincoln Town Car. She thought they conveyed luxury. Megan thought that was weird and she preferred the sporty cars. A Porsche or an older model Corvette really got her going.

"My mom's been dating this guy named George. He reminds me of a nerd, but she seems to be happy with him. I don't like him, and I haven't been too nice to him." Amy said.

"Treat him like dirt," Megan said. "Then he'll break up with your mom and you won't have to worry about him anymore. Most men don't date women with kids to begin with, especially bratty kids. I've caused a few dicks to break up with my mom."

"How mean!" Amy exclaimed, but she was laughing too. "I guess he's not really a *dick*. I don't know. It's nice to see Mom kind of happy, even if she is clueless. Maybe I'll start being human to him."

"You're such a geek sometimes Amy!" Laughed Megan as she hung her arm around Amy's shoulders. "And I'm so glad I could help you see the light in this situation."

"Yeah? Kiss my ass Megan!" It was fun using curse words.

"Kiss mine first!" Both girls were laughing and being typical young teens.

The sun was low, but it would be at least another hour before their moms arrived home from their jobs. As they came back around the block towards Amy's house, they were nearing the home of the Yard People. The big boy that lived there was in the yard.

"Don't you think that guy's kind of strange?" Amy asked Megan, then said quickly "Don't look at him."

"Yeah, but harmless. I think he's just slow or sort of retarded." Megan answered.

"We call them the Yard People because they always visit with their company outside in their yard." Amy said. "Not that they get much company. It's just the same ol' poor-looking people. If it's more than one, they're in a old ugly car, but sometimes it's just one of them, and he might be in an old pickup truck. Anyway, the house must be really grungy inside since no one ever goes in."

As they walked closer to the house the boy was slowly approaching them.

"Hello." he said slowly. He stood there with both feet planted and his arms hanging down, not moving at all – like dead weight standing. He had an innocence about him that seemed to be tainted somehow. Amy didn't feel afraid of him, yet there was an uncertainty.

"Want to... see my brother?" the boy asked quietly. "My brother wants... visitors." He seemed to have trouble finding his words.

"Brother?!" Amy blurted out. *I've never seen a brother! Or even a mother.* She thought. "How old is your brother?"

Stunned for a moment, the boy then said "Mark... is older than me. Come see him."

Mark had not been your typical teen. He had a brilliant mind for academics, but he was also a genuinely nice person. He had loved spending time with his little brother. Kevin was a pure joy to him, especially after being an only child the first nine years of his life. Not that being an only child was bad, Mark could always find ways to entertain himself, but he seemed to be happier when he was sharing his time with someone. His dad had always been busy with his medical practice and trying to keep their mom happy. He didn't have a lot of time for Mark. Mark's mother was the type that never seemed to be satisfied. She was too impatient most of the time, and since Mark was so independent, she basically left him alone. Kevin was bright and cheerful and full of wonder at the things his big brother could show him. There was an immediate bond between the two.

That bond became twisted over the last ten years as Mark existed in his lonely void. The affection towards Kevin turned into an obsession with mixed feelings of love and bitterness. Then eventually the love disappeared and all that was good in Mark became sour. He was mastering the power of his mind now and mastering Kevin's mind too.

Amy knew she shouldn't go with the boy into that house, but her curiosity got the better of her. Megan was all too willing to go in, which also emboldened Amy. As they approached the front stoop an odd feeling came over her, and then they entered. The house had a stale smell and it was gloomy. Then they entered Marks room. Amy felt sick when she saw the young man in the bed. His head, which had a greasy look to it, seemed way too big for his body. *His body.* Amy felt such pity. It was almost like nothingness under the bed covers. And then his *eyes.* He had to roll them way over to the side to look at her and Megan. The way those pitifully strained, dark brown eyes looked at her, it was like they were drawing her into his soul. The hissing-clicking sound of his oxygen machine was hypnotic.

15

When Linda came home from work, Amy was on the couch and neither the television nor the stereo was on.

"Hey Baby" Linda said. "How was your day?"

Amy looked up at her mother and just shrugged. She didn't say anything.

"Are you okay?" Linda asked. Still no response. "Amy. Why are you so quiet?" Did something happen today?"

"I don't think so." Amy replied, but she didn't sound convincing.

"What do you mean? Wouldn't you know if something happened that upset you?"

"I can't remember." Linda noticed a tear streaming down Amy's right cheek.

"What? Why?! What's wrong with you?" No response. "Amy, what did you do this afternoon?" Linda demanded.

"Mom, I'm not sure. I don't feel very good. Can I just go lay down?"

Linda reached over a placed her hand on Amy's forehead. No fever. No clamminess. "Go ahead, Baby. But we're going to talk about this when you do feel better."

What the hell has she been doing? Linda couldn't stand it. As much as she didn't want to, she called Megan's mother.

"Hi Connie. This is Linda, Amy's mom. I..."

"I'm glad you called." Connie interrupted. "What in the world have Megan and Amy been up to? Megan's walking around here like a goddam space cadet! I can't get her to make any sense!"

Now Linda was really worried. She was about Amy's age when she first tried smoking pot. *But Amy's not like me. She's got more discipline than I had. We've had all the talks... shit!* "That's why I called you Connie. Amy's not acting right either, and I can't get any answers out of her. I thought maybe something happened that might have upset her. Megan hasn't said anything?"

"Hell no. She's gone to lay down." Connie said. She was sounding a little calmer now. Connie wasn't so belligerent these days, but she always spoke her mind unfiltered. "I wish I knew, but I think our little girls are head-tripping on something. God knows, I've done enough drugs in my day that I think I know the signs!"

Linda was feeling exasperated. "Well, it's obvious we can't talk to them now. I'm going to get off the phone, but I would like to talk more about this when we know more. Bye now, Connie." Linda felt drained when she got off the phone. Amy was always such a good, easy child. She was never a problem as a baby or a toddler. Linda always feared the teenage years would be rough – hell she had to expect problems at some point. No parent was that lucky. *But this is too soon! She's only thirteen.*

Amy slept through the night, and not much was said between the two the next morning. Typically they were too busy scrambling to get to work and school on time for chatter, and this morning was no different.

Linda marched straight to Karen's office upon arriving to work. "I think Amy got high with her little friend Megan yesterday." she announced.

"Amy? No way Linda." Karen responded. "She's not like that, and you know it."

"That's what I thought... think... I just know I'm really worried. Megan's a little on the wild side, and you know how Amy feels about me dating. Anyway, she was in a real stupor last night. I couldn't talk to her, or rather she couldn't talk to me. And Connie, Megan's mom, said Megan was the same way. She thinks it's drugs for sure. Do you think Amy would do it to get back at me for dating George?"

"I thought she had more sense than that, but I also know how peer pressure can be." Karen said. "Try not to jump to any conclusions until you've talked with her. If it really is drugs, if you want, I'll talk to her. She thinks I'm pretty cool, right?"

"Yeah. She really does." Linda replied. "I may take you up on that, Karen. Thank you."

Linda had a hard time concentrating on work for most of the morning. "Michael," Linda buzzed his office just before lunch, "I think I'll take this afternoon off if it's alright with you."

Michael replied "That's fine. I may call you though, if I get in a bind."

Be sure to turn the phone off. Linda was reminding herself as she was leaving the office.

16

When Linda got home, she laid down on the couch to catch fifteen minutes. Sometimes just fifteen minutes of uninterrupted slumber made a world of difference. She awoke after ten minutes to the phone ringing. *Damn I forgot to turn it off!*

Hesitantly, she got up and answered, "Hello?"

"Hi Linda, it's George. I called your office and the receptionist said you'd gone home for the day."

"Uh-huh" she responded, trying not to sound annoyed.

"Did I wake you up? You sound fuzzy. You're not sick, are you?"

"Yes, you did and no, I'm not sick, I'm fine. What's up?"

"I'm sorry for waking you, I know how aggravating that is. Anyway, I'd like to take you to the Oyster Festival in Swansboro this weekend. Sound like fun?"

"Yes, it does." Linda replied smiling. "George, let's bring Amy with us."

"No problem, if you think she'll want to go. Most teenagers don't want to be seen with adults." He laughed. "Not to mention how she feels about me."

"I know she's been a little shit to you George, and I'm sorry. I just think she's going through something right now and I need to be more attentive to her. She's really a great kid. I hope you'll see that side of her soon. But thank you, and I love oysters! I'm looking forward to it."

"Good. We'll leave around 10:30 Saturday morning. But I would like to have you all to myself Friday night for dinner."

Linda was trying to think of what to do about Amy. "Okay. I'll see you Friday night."

I really like having George in my life, Linda was thinking. *But I don't like the separatism. Why can't we be more like a family? Why do I have to split my time between my child and my boyfriend? (Is he my boyfriend?) I do deserve time alone with George and I know a lot of families that spend less quality time with their kids than I spend with Amy.* She was trying to justify her new lifestyle and shed the guilt. She always felt she had raised Amy as good on her own as she could have with a husband, but now she was beginning to have doubts. *And what am I going to say to Amy when she comes home from school? Yesterday really threw me for a loop.*

Linda walked out onto the front porch. It was cool, but the sun was bright. Most of the hardwood trees were barren now and yards were deep with dried leaves. She wouldn't rake until all the leaves had dropped. No sense in doing it more than once. Things looked quiet next door. No visitors. *Should I go over and introduce myself? Have I put it off too long?*

Linda walked around to the side of her house pretending to inspect the paint or whatever home owners inspect on their homes. She kept glancing over at the Yard People's house. She finally mustered up the courage to go over. She walked up the front stoop and hesitated before knocking. Then, as she stood there with her arm raised up ready to knock, a strange feeling came over her. She couldn't bring herself to knock. She was feeling, *what was it? Disoriented? Confused?* Then a sort of panic crept up within her. She was running home before she even realized it. Once she was back in her own house, she felt very foolish. Linda looked out the window to see if anyone was around that might have seen her. *What the hell was that all about?* Linda decided she was *not* going to introduce herself to her neighbors. Etiquette called for them to introduce themselves to her. That was customary in her book.

Linda had taken the afternoon off so she could be there when Amy got home from school. And since she was home in the middle of the day, why not do something domestic? Linda put a load of clothes in the washing machine and looked for something to bake. It would be nice for Amy to come home to some fresh baked cookies or something. *Who are you kidding Linda? First you have to run to the grocery store and buy something to bake.* She did just that. There was a small grocer just minutes away, so she picked up some pre-made cookie dough that comes in a roll, she and Amy loved those kinds of cookies, and a carton of skim milk. Linda would have a batch of cookies baking in the oven when Amy arrived home and still have some unbaked for Amy to help with. It would be fun, and it was the closest to homemade Linda could handle. Amy liked to refer to this kind of activity as 'homesteading'.

When Amy arrived home from school, she could smell the sweet aroma of cookies baking. "Mmm, what smells so good?" she called out, wondering why her mother was home this early.

"Come in here and help me finish baking these cookies." Linda replied from the kitchen.

Amy felt a little timid, she was still uneasy about the previous day. But the aroma of cookies made her feel more at ease. "Yum. Oh, you got the fun kind!" she said happily.

"Yeah, I wanted to spend the afternoon with you. I feel like I've neglected you somehow since moving here. As for yesterday, well, do you feel like talking about it?"

"Mom, I wish I knew what happened to me. I've been trying to figure it out all day. And Megan's no help. She can't remember anything either, but she doesn't seem worried about it. Go figure."

"Please be honest with me Baby. Have you and Megan been trying pot or something? I know Megan's a little wild."

"Mom, no!" Amy answered defensively. "I'm not like that! I wish it was that simple. I just feel like I've lost some time somehow and it's really scaring me." Her voice beginning to crack as she fought back tears. "And please stop being so down on Megan. She's not a bad person, she's just not as inhibited as most. She doesn't live inside the little box everyone tries to keep us in."

Good for Amy sticking up for her friend thought Linda. "Okay, I'm sorry. I had to ask. What *do* you remember about yesterday?" Linda asked as she pulled a pan of cookies from the oven.

"I remember some of the boring stuff from first period, I remember going to lunch and I wasn't impressed with what they served, but I can't think of what it was, *then* I remember you coming home from work. Mom, I'm afraid. Do I have amnesia? I almost got points taken away from me at school today because I forgot to do my homework! I lied to the teachers because I didn't want to sound stupid or crazy. I told them we were at the hospital all night with a sick relative." Amy then got quiet and was sitting at the kitchen table with her head in her hands. Then she looked up at her mom, "Please don't be mad about the lie. And I'm going to make up the homework tonight."

"Do you feel alright today?" In spite of the situation, Linda felt pride in realizing Amy knew how to cover her ass at school, but she was so very worried about the lapse in Amy's memory. She knew she had to hide her fear so Amy could settle down.

"Yeah, other than confused, I'm fine."

"I honestly don't know what to make of this, Amy. They say stress can do strange things, and maybe the move from

Grandma & Grampa's was harder on you than we thought. Hopefully this is an isolated incident, but if it ever happens again, you need to let me know right away. We'll go see a doctor." Linda was rubbing Amy's back, "Don't let it trouble you anymore. Let's enjoy these cookies now, while they're warm. You want milk or black coffee?"

"Black coffee. I love you, Mom."

17

By now, Mark James had not only mastered the capability to absorb Kevin's memories, but, because this absorption process left Kevin's mind so frail, he was also able to control Kevin's thoughts and direct his actions.

Mark had given up on utilizing his father's mind a long time ago – it was far too depressing. Most of Dr. James' thoughts and memories were of self-loathing, pity and guilt over Mark and what had become of him. Some of his memories were of his domineering wife, who, coming from a poor family, had let her husband's income and status ruin what personality she once had. Mark didn't like remembering his mother that way.

Dr. James' depression over Mark had caused him to quit his medical practice, which lead to their meager existence. Social Security and Disability were their only means of income these days. He hated himself for not having the fortitude to forge ahead and continue being a productive man. He hated selling the big house that had been in his family for generations. He knew Mark should have been receiving the best medical attention that the son of a doctor could receive. Instead, he was withering away. And Dr. James didn't quite know what to make of Kevin. Kevin was so bright when he was younger. Dr. James hated himself for being weak, and it only made him weaker.

Friends and colleagues had long faded away, as they eventually do when tragedy strikes. Dr. James had no family to speak of. Only family members from his wife Leanne's side would visit sporadically, but they would never enter house. They didn't understand what was happening, but after experiencing some episodes of 'lost time' and seeing how Kevin and Clayton had become, they just knew to stay out of the house. They would visit, mostly out of curiosity and a lack of better things to do. But they always stayed outside, and had eventually resorted to just staying in their vehicles. They would find it in their hearts to bring prepared food occasionally. They cared about Kevin, but they weren't sure about Mark. They resented Clayton James though; he had been their only hope of pulling their family up out of the drudges, and now he was no better off than they.

Kevin, for a while however, was young and still able to find excitement from new experiences. But Kevin didn't venture out much anymore because his mind had become so dulled. All he really had now besides the occasional visit from relatives was his basic instincts and day to day drudgery. Mark had to make Kevin seek outside stimuli, but he had no idea where this would eventually take him.

When Mark directed Kevin to get Amy and Meagan to come in the house, his basic instincts really kicked in. The young pretty girls stirred up something in Mark he had long forgotten. Poor Kevin didn't remember any of it because Mark was relishing in the erotica. All the glory of Kevin's masturbation was his. He was envisioning the pretty girls being nude and in provocative positions, and then the ultimate climax of Kevin's early, but explosive orgasm — it was almost more than Mark could handle. He was finally feeling alive! It was more than he had ever hoped for! He was grateful that over the past few years he had revived his near-dead mind with the stolen memories of others, but he had never expected to *feel* the sensation of physical pleasure through stolen memories!

Mark's gradual disregard for other people had come full circle. His sole purpose was to nurture his own feeble existence no matter the cost to anyone else. And what he wanted now was some more sexual stimulation. He would have to concentrate hard to project his mind into Kevin's to achieve this, because what Mark now wanted was against Kevin's true nature. But Mark was confident because Kevin, like his dad, had become weak, therefore pliable.

18

The outing at the Oyster Festival was great. In Linda's mind the weather could not have been more perfect. It was cool and overcast with a slight breeze. Crisp, dried leaves were dancing around, and there was no blinding low sun in their eyes. Amy and George got to know each other a little better and both seem more relaxed. Amy even gained a little respect for George over their mutual passion for soft-shelled crabs.

They caught up with Karen and Richard at one of the game booths, which was a nice surprise. The five of them hung out together at the festival for the rest of the day, enjoying steamed oysters, live music and booths filled with arts and crafts, featuring local artisans. Festivals in Eastern North Carolina were quite an experience for all the senses. Linda fell in love with a pottery piece that George was all too happy to buy for her, and Amy was thrilled to take home a tie-dyed tee shirt.

19

Halloween had been uneventful. Amy was looking forward to passing out candy to little neighborhood goblins, but none showed up. The neighborhood was older, so alas, were most of its residents.

November did not disappoint though. The fall foliage was extra colorful this year, something Eastern North Carolina is not always privileged to see. The leaves on the big shade tree in Linda's back yard were a beautiful vibrant yellow and they were carpeting her yard in yellows and tans. The colors were beautiful in contrast with the deep blue Autumn sky.

Linda, Amy and George were gathering and packing up food they had been preparing, baking and cooking all morning to take over to Linda's parents' home for Thanksgiving. Together the three of them had cooked up some candied yams (canned) with some extra ingredients, apple pie (frozen) and a green bean casserole, actually home-made and not the kind with cream-of-mushroom soup. This was made with green beans, pre-fried bacon, tomatoes, onions, mushrooms and cheddar cheese. They all felt quite proud of themselves. This would be the first meeting between George and Linda's parents. Thanksgiving is Linda's favorite family holiday, and she was counting on her parents to be on good behavior.

Just as they were about to leave the house the doorbell rang. George answered the door to find a large boy standing on the front porch. It was Kevin.

"I want Amy to come over." was all he said. He had sweat beads on his forehead and upper lip, which George thought was very strange for how cool it was outside. Linda looked over George's shoulder.

"What?" she asked.

"I want Amy to come over." he repeated.

"Aren't you the boy from next door?" Linda asked. Kevin just stood there looking uneasy. "How do you know Amy? Answer me!" Linda was getting upset.

George calmly said to the boy "You need to go home. This is Thanksgiving. Go home now."

Kevin left without another word. "That boy's not right, is he?" George asked.

"I don't know. I don't think any of them are right." Linda said. "Amy, how does that boy know you?" she demanded.

"He doesn't know me." Amy replied. "I think he's creepy though."

"I hope he hasn't been looking at our mail when we're not here. But we don't get much mail with your name on it. This is weird." Linda's mind was going into overdrive.

"Look, he's gone." said George. "We don't have to think about it now. Let's just go."

Thanksgiving at Jim and Sharon's was fun. Linda and her mom enjoyed a little wine buzz. There was no real drama, just some subtle insults passed back and forth between Linda's parents. Sharon was still very beautiful – she was gorgeous in her youth. Amy was taking after her and Linda took after her father Jim, in coloring and in height. Jim and Sharon could get along wonderfully at times, but those times were getting fewer and further between. Lately, or for the past ten or so years now, they seemed to just bicker and pick at each other. Maybe it has something to do with getting older, or maybe they're just tired of each other. George got a real kick out of it.

"I'm glad you find it amusing." Linda said to George when they got back to Linda's house.

"Maybe that's just their way of keeping it spicy." George laughed and winked.

"Believe me, it can get old. I have to give them credit though, they were on pretty good behavior today. And Dad sure can cook a turkey! I'm so full still.... let's all take naps like we're supposed to."

By seven PM the house was dark and nothing could be heard but faint snores in three different keys.

20

BUZZZZ! "That goddam doorbell" Linda was muttering as she was trying to find the light. She looked out the peep hole. *Shit! What's he doing here again?!* It was Kevin on the porch. George was up by now. "George, this has to stop. Will you say something to him?" Linda pleaded.

George took care of the matter in more ways than one. Not only did he get rid of Keven, but he returned to Linda's house the next morning with a hand gun – a thirty-eight Smith & Wesson revolver, and some bullets. Then there was the lecture about always locking the windows and doors, always using the peep hole, always keeping the gun loaded, and to finish, he took Linda and Amy to his shop for lessons on gun safety, then how to shoot, and then some target practice. A Man's World was closed for the Thanksgiving holiday, so George was able to spend a lot of time with them. He was very protective (*almost paranoid?*) and very thorough.

Maybe George's love for guns does have some merit. Linda was starting to feel a little safer, although she couldn't exactly justify her fears. Kevin was just a slow-witted boy. But there was always that nagging feeling, that *something* about that family, the Yard People. Linda was now feeling more than just uncomfortable about them.

Linda was using her new thirty-eight revolver, and George had picked out a twenty-two automatic for Amy to practice with. The twenty-two was lighter, easier to handle with little recoil, and it held a lot of bullets. The thirty-eight only held six bullets, but they were a heavier caliber and the gun had to be manually cocked before firing. Linda was leery, yet excited.

"Damn!" Linda exclaimed. "I can't believe how loud this thing is, even with the ear muffs on!"

George was shooting with his forty-five revolver that he always kept with him. He hadn't shot in a while and was enjoying it. He had been very patient explaining all about the gun's components, safety measures, how to load, aim and so on, before they got started. Linda was impressed with his accuracy and speed, but even more impressed with Amy's.

"This is so cool." Amy said. She was shooting rapidly with an almost smug look on her face. Linda wasn't sure how to react to that. Guns had never been a part of their lives. When she noticed how well Amy was hitting the target, and not shooting wild, she felt somewhat better. George was surprised too.

"She's a natural. With some practice she could go into competition. I could work with her." he said.

"Oh Mom! Could I?" Amy was delighted.

Linda said "That's certainly something to think about. We'll see if you stay interested. This is just our first time, after all." *Jesus Christ*, she was thinking. *Going from no gun, to one gun, and now maybe I'll have to get my baby a gun?* It was all too much for her today. She was none too thrilled with her own shooting capabilities. "All I can do with a gun is nick someone just enough to piss them off."

"You *are* kind of rough with a gun." George replied reluctantly. He could see that Linda's arm was starting to tremble. They had been at it for almost forty-five minutes. "I don't know about y'all, but I've worked up an appetite. How about we go get some food?"

George decided he would switch the thirty-eight revolver at Linda's house with a twenty-two automatic. He figured Linda could more easily handle the twenty-two, and if it really came down to it, Amy would be the protector.

They ate at a little diner near George's shop that served a killer hot hamburger plate, which is what Amy and George both ordered. Linda was happy with a club sandwich. Amy and George did most of the talking during lunch that afternoon. Linda hadn't seen Amy this excited over something in quite a while. She was glad to see it, and could tell it was also another bonding of sort between the two.

21

"I love Christmas shopping!" Linda exclaimed as she and Amy were driving over to the mall. Linda was all smiles with her head bopping to the upbeat Christmas music playing on the radio. There was a local radio station that played Christmas music 24/7 from the day after Thanksgiving until the end of Christmas day.

"Mom, have you lost your mind?" asked Amy. "Nobody loves Christmas shopping."

"I do." Linda replied. "Always have. I love the crowds, well, if you can call it a crowd here in New Bern. I don't think I'd really like the big city crowds. I love the lights, choosing just the right gift, everything! You know how much I love to shop anyway; Christmas just gives me an excuse. I wonder what to get for Mom and Dad? They're starting to have too many things in their house now – I should think practical, which is not nearly as much fun."

"How about thinking *personal* instead of practical, like bath things or clothes?" Amy suggested.

"Yeah, you're right, Amy. How'd you get so smart?" Linda laughed. "Except clothes for Mom is out. But the toiletries idea is good, and she loves to read, so books are always good too. Dad could use a new everyday cardigan. His brown one is getting kind of raggedy." *But he sure loves that old brown cardigan.*

Linda was humming Christmas carol tunes as they entered the shopping mall. At first, they were just walking along, taking in the decorations and trying to decide which store to explore first. Then Linda spotted Bitchy Niki walking towards them. *Oh, that woman! I can't imagine the Christmas spirit hitting her!* Then all of a sudden, the devil flew into Linda – and she did something very out of character.

"Hey, Niki!" she called, waving. Niki looked her way, no smile or acknowledgment of any kind, but she did come over.

"Merry Christmas." Linda said overly cheerful.

"Thank you." Niki replied dryly. Linda detected a minute smirk on the corner of Niki's mouth.

"Look, I have these neighbors. It seems like something's not right with their electrical hook-up." *I can't believe I'm telling this bald-face lie!* "They have this big wire attached to a pole behind their house that runs alongside and into their house. Does that sound right to you?" Linda asked with a quizzical look on her face, knowing full well that this would peak Nikki's attention.

Linda had to contain herself when she actually saw some life coming into the bitch's eyes.

"Mom, what..." Amy started to ask.

Linda quickly interrupted her with "Amy, go over to the ice cream shop and order us two cones. You know what I like so go ahead now." as she nudged Amy away. "And I'll be right there Baby!" she called as Amy was walking off.

"Are you telling me your neighbor is stealing electricity?" Niki asked wide-eyed. Linda knew that Niki would just love to bust someone and then bask in the glory.

"Well, I don't know if that's what's going on. I just thought it was odd because it's been that way since before I moved there, and it seems kind of dangerous, especially when it rains. They could have a fire hazard and not even realize it. So, I thought I should mention it to you." Linda was feigning concern. "Anyway, you have a nice holiday if I don't see you before Christmas. Bye now."

What have I done? Linda was feeling giddy like a school girl. She wasn't the type to play pranks, but for some reason she wanted Niki to go by the Yard People's house. *Why? Maybe I'd better...* She turned back around but couldn't see Niki anywhere in sight. Now she wasn't feeling so fun anymore. She was feeling quite ashamed of herself. *What could happen? It's a harmless hoax, Niki will just be made a fool of, and she deserves it.* Linda was attempting to justify her childish prank.

The mall was so pretty and festive with all the decorations and the Christmas music playing. There were people everywhere! Some all bundled up and looking flustered. Linda loved the busy shopping weekend after Thanksgiving. As she approached the ice cream parlor, she saw that Karen and Richard had found Amy. The three of them were sitting together having ice cream, Amy holding two cones.

"Mom, I got your Chocolate Espresso cone." Amy said. "Who was that mean-looking lady you were lying, ahem, I mean, talking to?"

Karen shot Linda a quizzical look.

"That was the lady from building inspections you've heard me complain so much about. Man, I finally did something to make her happy, the wicked bitch." *I really shouldn't talk this way in front of Amy.*

"Why in hell would you want to make *her* happy?" Karen asked, looking perplexed.

"I wasn't actually trying to make her happy," Linda said, "but you know her type, someone else's plight is her pleasure."

Now Richard was interested. "What are you talking about? What did you say to her?" He asked, with ice cream on his nose.

Linda looked down, kind of ashamed but giggling too. "I told her a lie." She explained what she told Niki. "I just wanted to see if she would investigate," then looking up, "She jumped on it like stink on shit! Don't ask me why I did it. For some reason I want her to go to my neighbor's house and snoop around, and she can't hardly wait to do it. That's how mean she is. She won't find anything; I mean nothing they could get in trouble for." The more Linda talked the more she realized she'd screwed up.

"Wow - don't mention this to Michael. If our permits start getting held up I don't want him to know it's because of some stupid prank I pulled on Niki." Linda's ice cream had started dripping down her hand, and she knew she need to stop talking now. She took a deep breath and started in on her Chocolate Espresso cone.

Richard and Amy ate their ice cream in silence, as they were silently judging Linda.

"That's pretty funny though." Karen said. "I wish I could've seen her face light up when you told her. Better yet, I'd like to be there when goes to 'bust' those... Linda, are you sending her to the Yard People?"

"None other." said Linda, trying to appear clever but her guilt was beginning to show.

"Man, she's going to catch them getting high. You better hope doesn't use your name." Karen was worried then. She assumed the Yard People were pot smokers because of how Linda had described them and their friends.

"So. She's not a cop. Hell, she's not even a building inspector. What can she do but make a fool of herself for impersonating an inspector" Linda said. "I'm not worried." that wasn't true. Linda was feeling guilty and worried, but she tried hard to not let it show. "Amy, you realize this isn't 'role model' behavior, right?"

Amy replied "Give me some credit, Mom. But I hope she *does* find something wrong, and makes those creepy people move."

"So, Richard," Linda was changing the subject. "Is this *The* Christmas? Shopping in any jewelry stores this year?"

"Get real, woman!" Richard replied laughing.

"What about you and George?" Karen quipped. "I hardly see you anymore since Richard hooked you up with that old fart." Amy busted out laughing at this.

"Hey now!" said Linda. "Anyway, old farts don't smell as bad a fresh ones." Then she laughed at her own joke.

"Y'all are so gross!" cried Amy. "It's like I'm the adult here today!" Everyone started laughing at that, then calmed down to enjoy their ice cream cones and watch shoppers.

After a short while Amy said, "George is teaching us to shoot guns, and he says I'm a natural."

Karen and Richard just looked at Linda and Amy, not quite knowing what to say.

"You know," Linda said, "he has that shooting gallery behind his shop. We just went yesterday for the first time, and Amy *was* good. Don't look so stunned. We're not turning into rednecks. George is just the type who believes people should know how to protect themselves. It's not such a bad idea. He gave us a gun to keep at the house, and he's taught us about safety."

"Linda," Karen said, "guns can be more trouble than they're worth. I don't want you guys getting hurt. And what if one of Amy's friends finds it?"

"Amy's had all the lectures. She knows the dangers and knows to leave it alone – she'll only practice with supervision. Please don't worry, I actually feel safer having it." Linda said. Once again, she wanted to change the subject, but it would be awkward.

Richard saved her. "Let's start some shopping. You girls drug me out here, now let's get it over with." he said.

"Yeah, it'll be fun." Linda added. "Too bad it's not snowing."

"Thank God it's not snowing!" Karen said. "Let's get our parents done first. Mine are hard to shop for."

After about three hours of Christmas shopping, Richard was on the brink of insanity. And he had no escape either because he rode with Karen.

22

Meanwhile, Megan had wanted to hang out with Amy. Her mom was working, so Megan left her house that Saturday morning shortly after eleven and started strolling through the neighborhood towards Amy's house. She didn't mind the cold and she was taking her time. The neighborhood seemed so quiet and lonely. Most people were either shopping or still visiting their out-of-town families. When she got to Amy's she noticed Linda's car wasn't in the driveway, but she didn't think anything of it. She went up onto the front porch and rang the doorbell. After no answer, she walked around to the back of the house. She stopped under Amy's bedroom window, "Amy!" she hollered. "Get up and answer the door, you lazy turd!"

When she got no response, she started back around to the front and was was startled by Kevin. She gasped when she looked up into his confused eyes. Her heart started racing before her legs had a chance to, and before she could think or run, Kevin grabbed her up into his huge arms and was carrying her off to his house. He covered her mouth so she couldn't cry out. He was breathing hard although he was moving slowly with her.

Megan felt completely helpless as she struggled hopelessly and this awful feeling of dread was washing over her.

Kevin, too, was feeling helpless. His actions were not his own, but he pressed on. He got her into his house and then into his bedroom. He threw her onto the floor with his full weight upon her as he started grappling at her body and trying to tear her clothes away. Megan could hardly catch her breath under his weight, but managed to kick something over, a lamp maybe, that made a crashing noise.

"God in Heaven!" Dr. James cried as he entered the room. "Kevin! Stop this!" He managed to pull Kevin away and Megan scrambled into a corner on the floor and started crying hysterically. Kevin stumbled out of the room and Dr. James just stood there, bewildered, staring hopelessly at Megan.

Mark however, he was taking it all in. Damn his father for spoiling his erotic adventure! But what a thrilling adventure it was while it lasted. Even the terror in Megan. He was absorbing everything.

Slowly Megan began to calm down. Not because she felt safe, but because she was already forgetting what had taken place. She still felt the residue of terror, but she couldn't rationalize it. Somewhere in the background she could hear Dr. James's pacing heavily and muttering loudly but it was incomprehensible. She found her way out of the house and made her way back to Amy's front porch. And there she sat, alone and disoriented, not even realizing her shirt was ripped.

"What has become of you? What have you created?" Dr. James was pulling at his thick white curls, pacing back and forth in Mark's room. "I can't let this go on. How could I let this happen?"

Mark looked so dead. But Dr. James knew it was him, the evil was emitting from his eyes. Those eyes. They rolled slowly in that lifeless head, attempting to follow his back-and-forth pacing.

23

Linda and Karen had accomplished quite a lot of their shopping, at least what they could while in the presence of Amy and Richard, who were becoming more baggage than what was in Linda's and Karen's shopping bags.

"I'll die if we don't stop and eat." Richard proclaimed. What he really wanted was a beer. "Amy must be famished too. You women are being oppressive. You know you have us trapped here in this mall."

"Fine, Whiner. We're finished anyway." Karen replied. "We wanted to go to the Bistro and have a couple of pitchers of beer and some sandwiches, but if you feel we must leave..."

"Oh Baby! I love the way you think!" Richard was all smiles again.

Karen laughed and winked at Linda. "Isn't he adorable?"

They headed to the Bistro, which was mostly a hangout for mall employees. It had great atmosphere and good food – what more could one ask for? And it was still in the mall. The four of them spent about an hour and a half there winding down, eating, drinking and wrapping up a busy day. Amy enjoyed being included with her mom's friends, but was happy to slip away with a pocket full of quarters (thanks to

Richard) to the corner of the Bistro where the video games were located.

It was dark by the time Linda and Amy got home. As they entered the house the phone was ringing.

"Hello?" Amy picked up.

"Put your mother on the phone." was the reply.

"Mom, it's for you." Amy said cupping the receiver and looking alarmed. "It sounds like Megan's mom."

Linda whispered, "What's her mother's name again? I can't think of it."

"Connie." Amy replied.

"Thanks." Linda cleared her throat. "Hi Connie. How..."

"Something happened to Megan today," Connie interrupted, "and I think it happened at your house!"

"What do you..." Again, Linda was cut off.

"Megan wasn't here when I got home from work, so I drove around looking for her. I found her sitting on your porch with her shirt torn and she was scared to death! I could tell she'd been crying, but she says she doesn't know how her shirt got torn. All she says is she's afraid. I want to know what the hell happened to my girl!" Connie's voice was breaking.

"Oh, Connie. I'm so sorry. But I can't help you, we haven't been home all day. We just now got in. She can't tell you anything? Is she in shock?" Linda was very concerned. This was all too familiar. A loud banging in her head kept telling her it was the Yard People. She felt the dread washing over her.

"I don't know. I don't know anything!" Connie was sobbing and shouting at this point. "She doesn't appear to be physically harmed, but... this doesn't make any goddam sense! She can't remember anything!" After a brief pause, "Look, I'm sorry. I think I'll take her to see the doctor on Monday. If there's a weirdo in the neighborhood, well, just watch out for Amy too. Goodbye." Connie hung up before Linda could say anything else.

24

George arrived at Linda's the following evening at close to seven PM. Linda was watching for him through the peephole while Amy was peering through the blinds. He got out of his truck and was coming up the walk to the porch.

"Oh, fuck me!" he suddenly blurted out as he jumped backwards about five feet, dropping his keys.

Linda and Amy burst out laughing. "It works Mom!" Amy exclaimed excitedly.

Lindy hurriedly opened the door. "It's okay George! I'm sorry, come on in." She was still laughing, holding her stomach.

Linda and Amy had gone out early in the morning to the concrete place out on US 70 East, just outside of town, where they sell birdbaths and other concrete yard décor. They bought a concrete statue of a Doberman Pinscher dog. It took both of them to lift it and lay it into the back seat of the car. They then hauled it to Karen's with some black and brown paint – Karen's quite talented with paint. Now they had this ominous looking dog sitting on their porch with a real collar and chain, and even food and water bowls for effect. Because of the shrubbery around the porch, it really couldn't be seen until one reached the porch steps.

"This is our intruder deterrent. He's maintenance-free, and now we know he works." Linda was all over herself with pride. "Isn't he great?"

"Until you get sued by someone for hurting themselves on your property." George answered somewhat pouty – his pride was hurt. But he soon pulled himself together. "Damn sure gave me a start! I guess it is a pretty good idea – funny actually." He was grinning now.

"Yeah, with that weird boy next door and whatever happened with Megan yesterday, I figured I needed to do something, and Fido here fits my budget." Linda had called George last night, after the Connie call, and told him about the episode with Megan.

Still a little embarrassed, George changed the subject. "So, did you girls have a good time shopping yesterday? I hope you spent all your money on me."

"It was fun." Amy said. "It wasn't just girls either. Karen's boyfriend Richard came too."

"I don't know how he stood it. I don't like all that shopping hassle." said George.

"You'd better start liking it, because I want some Christmas presents." Linda said, with authority, while batting her eyelashes at him. George felt something stir in him, and he was liking it.

"Me too!" Amy piped in. "Where's your Christmas Spirit?"

"It's in my truck. Come on." George headed back outside. He went to his truck and pulled out a big box filled with Christmas lights, outdoor extension cords and a staple gun.

Amy started hopping. "Oh wow! This is *so cool!* We've never had outside lights before, George! Thanks! Can I help put them up?" Linda couldn't remember seeing Amy this excited in a long time.

"I was hoping you would. We'll do it tomorrow though, when we can see." The sun had already set and it was almost dark. He brought the box in the house. "Right now, I want to go eat and maybe rent some movies."

Amy was on top of the world. She was feeling like a Hallmark family. Maybe it was the Christmas Spirit, but she hoped it would last. The three of them ate at a quiet little seafood restaurant and afterward rented a couple of movies from Blockbuster to watch at the house. Amy fell asleep about fifteen minutes into the second movie. George would be spending the night for the first time while Amy was at the house. They had discussed it over dinner, and she was fine with it. She knew he had stayed when she wasn't there. *How naive do they think I am?* She thought during the conversation.

The next morning, while in the kitchen having coffee, Linda was gazing out the window, or rather, watching. The Yard People. She watched while the poor-looking people sat in their old pickup truck. She saw the father talking to them, shaking his head. His gestures looked as though he was trying to reason with them about something. He went back in the house and the people in the truck looked like they were arguing somewhat. After a little while, the father and the boy came out. The boy was carrying a gym bag and got in the bed of the truck. *He's going with them! Maybe he'll stay with them for a while.* Linda felt relieved. The truck drove off and the father, looking distraught, just sat on his front stoop for a while before going back inside. *It's too cold to stay outside, you poor old man.* The caffeine was kicking in so Linda started gathering up items for preparing breakfast when George stumbled in for his coffee.

"Good morning, Babydoll." He said as he leaned down and kissed the back of her neck.

God, I love when he calls me that. Linda was smiling "I can make breakfast if you're hungry. Grits and bacon. Maybe the aroma will wake Amy up." she said.

"No hurry. I'll just have some coffee for now." He was already fixing himself a cup. Linda went to him and put her arms around his waist and rested her head on his back. He set his cup down and turned around to embrace her and she felt like she could stay there for an eternity.

Amy woke up to good, salty breakfast aromas. "I'm going to go see Megan after we eat." she said. "See how she's doing. I hope that's okay. I won't stay long, and then I'll help with the lights."

"That's a good idea." Linda replied. "We'll be ready to eat as soon as you're dressed and your face is washed. George, I need you to get out the butter and strawberry jam."

"Yes Ma'am." he replied, a little too quickly, which gave Linda just a fleeting moment of curiosity.

They had a good, relaxing breakfast and then Amy was out the door. "Don't linger on your way there, Amy!" Linda called to her while clearing the table, relieved that Megan's house was in the opposite direction of the Yard People's house.

George was still sitting at the table, and Linda walked up behind him and started massaging his thick, broad shoulders. He immediately closed his eyes and a small, satisfied smile came over his face. Linda was good with her hands and she knew it. George loved her strength. She kept it up as long as she could before she started becoming aroused. Then she slowly kissed the back of his neck and up and down the sides of his neck while she was still massaging. "Has your breakfast settled?" she whispered slowly into his ear before sucking on his earlobe, and then biting it.

"Oh yes Ma'am." George replied as he pulled her around into his lap and passionately kissed her mouth. *Again, with the Ma'am?* Linda wondered, but didn't let it deter her mood. "I'm hungrier now than before breakfast." George whispered back, kissing her throat, sending chills down her back and causing her breasts to harden and yearn for him. They both stood up, gazing into each other's eyes and their breathing was noticeably heavy. "The last one in bed does the dishes!" she blurted out and ran for the bedroom, laughing. George darted off behind her and they jumped into the bed and took advantage of the time they had to themselves.

25

Amy was in Megan's bedroom sitting with her on the bed looking over some CDs to play.

"Where were you yesterday?" Megan asked.

"We were Christmas shopping at the mall with Karen and Richard." After a pause Amy asked, "Are you alright? What happened to you yesterday?"

Megan looked at Amy for what seemed like a long time. Finally, she said, "I can't explain it, but something bad happened. You know how we had that day we couldn't explain, you know, we couldn't remember much about school that day and all? When my mom got all uptight and thought we were freaked out on drugs?"

"Yeah. That still bothers me." Amy said.

"Well, something like that happened again. But this time I felt afraid for a long time but I can't explain why. I vaguely recall seeing that weird neighbor of yours. And I'm pretty sure we saw him that other time too." Megan got quiet for a moment. Then she said, "You need to be really careful of him, Amy. I think he has powers or something. He's probably one of those devil worshipers, or voodoo freaks. I'm super serious, don't go near him." Megan was dead serious now. "I'm worried he might have done something to me and

83

I don't know what. But my top was torn when my mom found me sitting on your porch steps."

"Oh, Megan. I'm so sorry." Amy reached over and embraced Megan in her arms. She was getting scared. "That creep came up to our door one day to see me. I couldn't figure out why. Do you remember anything about him having a brother?"

Megan looked thoughtful. "Not until you just now mentioned it. Seems like there was…" Fragments of that day were starting to come into her memory. "I think he told us about a brother?" Megan and Amy just sat together in silence for a while.

26

Karen was humming to Muzak Christmas tunes in the office while she was decorating anything she could. Cindy was her helper, handing her the stapler and whatnot. Linda was tapping away at her desktop keyboard, stopping occasionally to admire(?) the tacky decorations. "I don't know if Michael's going to appreciate this." she said. "He might worry that our clients will look at it as a reflection of his work."

"Do you think so?" Karen asked innocently. "I like shiny, sparkly things. It's kind of a fifties retro vibe, don't you think?"

"How do you know what they did at Christmas in the fifties?" Cindy asked. "Aren't you a little young for that? Linda, is she right?"

"Go to hell Cindy." Linda laughed. *Damn, does she really think I'm that old?* "Have you never seen a Christmas movie from the 1950s?" *Since it's Karen's doing, Michael will get over it.* Linda was now on the phone waiting for someone from building inspections to answer.

"Manning here." she heard on the other end.

"Chief Manning?!" Linda was caught off-guard. "How nice to hear your voice. I wasn't expecting you to answer. Where's Niki?"

"Oh, she's off on some goose chase, and who's this?" Manning replied.

"This is Linda at Michael Angelo's. I'm calling to see if I can come by and pick up our permits for the Parker job."

"I should've known your voice, girlie. The inspections went just fine. Niki ought to have the paperwork done a little later today. Like I said, she's gone off on one of her investigations." Manning said the word *investigations* with a tone of sarcasm. "Says she got a hot tip over the holiday. I just hope she doesn't go trespassing anywhere, she's not authorized you know. But she assured me it was just a look-see."

"I see." said Linda. *Oh Fuck.* "I'll stop by some time after lunch then. You have a good day, Chief." Linda hung up the phone knowing exactly what Niki was up to. *I don't care if she is a bitch, I shouldn't have told her that story.* Linda was feeling nauseous from guilt.

"Let's go to the mall for lunch and do a little more shopping." Karen was calling from Michael's office, still decorating. "I saw this great parka I want to get for Richard. It's still supposed to be twenty-five percent off."

"That's fine." Linda called back, knowing damn well she should go home for lunch and check out the situation next door. "But you'll have to stop by building inspections with me afterward."

Karen said "Cool. I haven't had a stare-down with Bitchy Niki in a long time."

"Yeah, it might be interesting." Linda mumbled to herself under her breath.

Michael was due back in the office before lunch, which would be in a couple of hours. Linda busied herself with some blueprint revisions and Cindy went back to her desk in the front, but Karen continued decorating and humming.

Linda was just finishing up on the phone with a prospective client when Michael came in. She looked up at him as she was placing the receiver back in it's cradle, trying not to burst out laughing. He was standing there with his fists on his hips, looking around at all the silvery tinsel and sparkly doo-dads, and slowly shaking his head. Karen came out from her office with a huge smile on her face.

"This looks like shit." he finally said.

"Whoa, man." said Karen, looking hurt.

"Of course." Michael said looking at Karen. "This is *your* creation." Then he chuckled. "I guess I should be grateful you don't let loose like this with your draft-work."

The office was filled with metallic garlands of green, red and silver, large plastic light-up balls of every color, snowflakes on every window, and a big silver foil Christmas tree in the lobby decorated to the hilt including one of those old-time rotating color wheels underneath. All items Karen had collected from garage sales and bargain bins over the past several years.

"I knew he would love it!" Karen said excitedly. "Let's go to the mall now."

On their way to the car Karen confessed, "I love the shock value of pulling a stunt like that."

"Oh, don't I know." Linda was trying to sound enthused.

Lunch at the mall wasn't very satisfying. Anytime the mall is real busy, the service can't keep up and the food gets prepared too fast. But, it's the holiday season and that's just how it is. Karen got Richard's parka, but Linda couldn't decide what to get for George. He was still a little bit of a mystery to her. There was something about him she couldn't quite pinpoint. But she did find some things for Amy - some music CDs by Radio Head and Collective Soul, and a nice jacket. Linda and Karen went in together on a gift for Michael. They picked out some expensive cologne with a subtle fragrance, and a very nice pullover sweater. They knew he would be giving each of them, including Cindy, an extra week's salary and he would take all of them out to dinner - probably at the country club.

That afternoon, when Linda and Karen arrived at the building inspections office, Chief Manning was sitting at Niki's desk. Linda's heart sank.

"Hey, Chief." she said. "You know Karen, don't you?"

"We've spoke on the phone, but I haven't had the *pleasure* of meeting you in person." he replied, looking Karen up and down. Her beauty took him off-guard. Then after a moment, "Anyway, I'm sorry your permits aren't processed yet, Linda. Niki never came back. She took off at about nine-thirty and I haven't heard a word from her. She doesn't answer at home." His forehead wrinkled as he began to frown. "I have to tell you, I'm concerned."

Linda felt sick. Before she knew it, she was out the front door and into the small alley-way throwing up her mall lunch. Soon she felt Karen's hands holding her hair and her purse back. Karen handed her a tissue when she was sure she was finished.

"Linda?" Karen looked very puzzled.

"We have to go to my house." Linda said, crying. "I just know Niki went to see my neighbors because of what I told her. I just know she's in some kind of trouble, and it's all my fault!" Linda was really sobbing now.

Karen was trying to calm her. "Don't let your imagination do this. I'm sure there's a reasonable explanation why that witch didn't come back to work. But, of course, come on. I'll drive us on over there. Try to pull yourself together. You'll see, everything will be fine." But Karen was feeling apprehensive too, and not sure why.

27

About thirty miles to the west, out in the country near the small town of Dover, down a rural road in a small house not much different from Linda's. Kevin was sitting at a kitchen table having lunch with his frail yet stern-looking grandmother and his thin, dried-up looking uncle. Kevin felt odd to be away from home, although he was feeling better than he had for a very long time. He had more energy and was noticeably more alert. Even the food he was having for lunch, which was only fried bologna sandwiches with sliced tomatoes and sweet iced tea, tasted better to him than any food he'd eaten in a long time.

"This is delicious, Grandma." he said. "Is there more?"

"He's gonna eat us outta house and home. What'd I tell you?" his Uncle Carson was complaining to the old woman.

"Hush Carson. 'Course there's more, Kevin. I'll just fix you right up." Grandma replied. She got up, wiping back loose gray strands of hair that had slipped out of her pony tail away from her face and turned the fire on under the cast iron skillet. She got more bologna out of the small refrigerator. As she was frying up the bologna, she said, "I thought we might take in a movie this evening, if you want to, Kevin. There's an Arnold Schwartzen-somethin-or-nother movie playing at the theater in town. Would you like that?"

"I guess." Kevin answered uncertainly.

"He don't even know who that is, Ma. I bet he's never even been to the movies. At least not in a long time." said Uncle Carson. "Your cousin William loves those action movies. Remember? He's told you 'bout them."

Kevin remained silent, but curious.

"Damn shame the way this boy's been raised." Grandma was saying under her breath to no one in particular. "I know he's no idiot. Just that depressing environment he has to live in." Then she said, "Carson, hadn't you noticed how he's talking now more than he ever does when we visit?"

"Yeah." said Carson. "Their place gives me the shits. Old Man Clayton's just plain nuts, and I swear to Christ that place is evil..."

"Stop it!" Grandma interrupted. Carson had started using his loud voice and Grandma didn't want to upset Kevin. "It's still his family" she said quietly. "Try to be delicate if you know how."

"Movies are kind of like TV, aren't they?" Kevin asked.

"Only better, and bigger too." Uncle Carson calmly replied as he popped a top on a can of generic beer. "You'll like it, Kevin."

Kevin's cousin William would be home from school in a little while. Kevin was looking forward to that. William was fun. They were the same age and William knew neat things to do. He had already shown Kevin his secret places in the woods. One place was like a fort he and some friends had built. They kept dirty picture magazines out there. But mostly, William and his buddies played war games when they were in the woods. William even had a friend that had a cement pad in his back yard with a basketball goal. Kevin really enjoyed trying to get the ball in the net, and he wanted to learn more about that game.

Kevin had stopped going to school about three years ago. His school had no luck in communicating with his family, and for some reason, when a school official went to the house, nothing ever came of it. Kevin eventually fell through the cracks of the system, and now he was old enough for the school to no longer bother with him.

Grandma remembered when Kevin was a bright, enthusiastic child. She knew he was not retarded like everybody else thought. At one time he was smarter than her other grandson, William. It was only a few years after her dead daughter's husband lost everything he had, that Kevin started going into his shell (as she referred to it). But after spending a few days with Kevin away from his house, she could see some of his old self coming out.

Kevin's Grandma started thinking back with a smile on her face. She remembered when her daughter, Leanne, started going out with Clayton. He was a young doctor just out of medical school and working at the hospital in New Bern. Grandma never dreamed her girl would hook up with a doctor! It was strange how they met. A church picnic. Clayton's parents weren't very well off, Clayton was so smart he received all his schooling through scholarships. His family attended the same Free-will Baptist church as her family. Leanne was just out of high school, and so pretty. She was tall, with dark hair cut in into a pixie. Her skin was pale and she had deep blue eyes. She was wearing a periwinkle blue print sun dress on that day of the picnic. The young doctor couldn't help but notice her. He took a fancy to her right away, and they spent most of that afternoon together.

During their courtship Grandma made time to sew special outfits for Leanne to help make her even more attractive. She was determined to help out in any way to get her girl married to a rich doctor. When they finally married some two years later, Grandma thought all her prayers had been answered. Clayton had specialized in surgery, and was starting a practice of his own, and Leanne was making friends with some real high-falutin' women. Leanne didn't seem to have much time for her Ma anymore, but she did send money home regularly. Grandma noticed, too, that Leanne was changing. Spoiled, some would call it. Nothing seemed good enough for her sometimes. Clayton was starting to look tired and unhappy. But Grandma wasn't the type to interfere. She said nothing to her daughter about her behavior or her marriage – didn't want to "rock the boat".

When Leanne died in that awful car crash, Grandma thought she would lose her mind. She missed her baby girl, even though Leanne hadn't been much of a daughter to her for several years. She thought about how Kevin was so little and happy and curious. And her grandson Mark – he was the light of her life. He was so sweet and smart and full of love. How could God do this to him? Grandma often felt that her lust for money, the way she pushed her daughter to marry for money, let to this tragedy.

She was burdened with guilt as well as grief over Leanne and Mark. So now she decided she would make things right for Keven, at least she would try her best.

Grandma had to approach her son Carson gently about what she wanted. She decided she wanted Kevin to live with them always. The house was small, and she lived in it with Carson and his wife Sandy, and their son William. Carson was a house painter. He couldn't work if the weather was too cold, or too hot, or too wet, or too humid. That didn't leave much time for making money. He could have done other things, but he was lazy and not apt to change. Sandy worked at the chemical plant on the other side of Dover. The pay wasn't great, but the job did come with benefits and sometimes she got over-time. And then Grandma has her steady Social Security checks coming in. William and Kevin should be able to share a bedroom. She knew that Carson and Sandy already felt crowded with her there, but hell, it might be Kevin's only chance and he *is* family. She had some say in the matter because Carson and Sandy depended on her monthly checks. They would have to take Kevin back to his house for Christmas, but then after the holiday she would do what she could to get Carson, Sandy and Clayton, to agree on Kevin moving in permanently with them.

28

When Linda and Karen arrived on Linda's street, they saw Niki's white Malibu parked on the street in front of the house of the Yard People, and Niki was sitting in it. They pulled on around and into Linda's driveway. They both got out of Karen's SUV and walked over to Niki's car. She did not look at them, but just sat there, staring at the steering wheel in front of her.

"Niki?" Linda said.

Niki slowly turned her head and looked at Linda. There was no recognition in her eyes, which was not unusual, but neither was there any hatefulness or indifference.

"Niki, are you alright?" Karen asked.

"I think so." she replied and looked around with an uncertainty. "Where am I?"

"You're in my neighborhood. Why don't you come over to my house and we'll have some coffee." Linda offered.

After a pause, Niki smiled and replied, "Okay. Thank you, Linda."

Who ARE you? Linda thought as she opened Niki's car door and offered her a hand. Niki took it and stepped out. As they were walking to Linda's house, Karen and Linda both noticed the old "yard" man peering out his front window at them.

Niki was trying to compose herself. "I don't quite know why I'm here. What time is it? Wait, I was looking for a violation at your neighbor's, wasn't I? What time did you say it is?"

"It's Two-fifteen." Karen said, her eyes darting back and forth at Linda and Niki.

"Try to relax and enjoy your coffee." Linda said to Niki as she was setting a cup of coffee in front of her. Niki was now sitting with Karen at Linda's kitchen table. "I'm going to call Chief Manning and let him know you're alright. I'll tell him you need the rest of the day off."

"Yes. Thank you." Niki replied, very politely. "I have to tell you though, I feel very strange. I don't think I found any violations. I don't recall much, for some reason. But *I do* feel like I've had a heavy burden lifted. Isn't that strange?" Then looking at the two women she was having coffee with, "Aren't you both from Michael Angelo's?" she said as she was looking at Karen now.

Linda and Karen just nodded, trying to look friendly. Then Linda got up to make the call. *She's being so civilized. What's gotten in to her? She should be really pissed at me.* After a few moments she returned. "Chief Manning was very understanding. He's just relieved you're alright." Linda said as she sat back down with some Graham crackers on a plate. She knew Niki probably hadn't eaten anything all day.

Niki ate some of the crackers with her coffee, and after a little while decided she needed to go home.

"We'll follow you home." Karen said. And then to Linda, "And we need to get back to the office." Karen was looking hard at Linda searching for an explanation.

"Okay, Linda," Karen started as she drove, following Niki's car. "Just what the fuck is with these *Yard People?*"

"It's the damnedest thing." Linda replied. "It seems like people act weird, or different after they've been there. Oh my God!" she exclaimed suddenly. "Amy! I'll bet Amy had some kind of contact with them that day she was so confused. But she doesn't remember anything. And, you know, that one day I was going to meet them, I had a real strange feeling come over me, just standing on their porch!"

"Wait a minute. You never told me that." said Karen feeling alarmed.

"No, I guess I didn't." she answered. "It was kind of embarrassing. I never talked to any of them. I started to knock on their door when I began to feel disoriented or something. I panicked and ran home and said to hell with it."

"Damn, that is screwed up. I don't think they did any harm to Niki though." said Karen.

"Yeah. I've never seen her so... nice?" Linda looked confused. "This whole neighbor thing as gotten just too weird. The thing about Megan, though, that has me worried. And that boy coming over to the house for Amy? I really don't know what's going on over there, and maybe I shouldn't know, but I do know to stay away from there and to keep Amy away. The boy is gone for now, I think he's staying with those folks that visit in their cars."

"That's good that he's gone. So, what do you think Michael will say about our extended lunch hour?" Karen was making a 'yikes' face.

Linda smirked. "To be honest, I don't think he'll notice. Cindy's probably aggravated with us though."

29

Earlier that morning when Niki was at the home of the Yard People, she had gone around the back looking for the drop cord connected to the light pole. Of course, she found nothing, but that wasn't good enough. She decided to knock on the front door to inquire about it. Upon Dr. James opening the door, Niki's mind got really fuzzy. She went inside though, unknowing that it was Mark drawing her in, because that's something she never would have done. Dr. James certainly didn't ask her to come in. He basically ignored her and went into the kitchen. Strangers would come by once in a while, and since Kevin wasn't home, he didn't want to be bothered. Niki found her way into Mark's room. Mark realized right away he was not interested in any of her memories. Nothing of interest there. However, there was *something*. Besides his own, he had never experienced such hatred. This woman was like a cesspool of abhorrence and resentment bubbling over, and he was absorbing it all. Every bit. So, because of his encounter with Niki, he was now pure, unadulterated evil.

30

It was the weekend now and Linda and George were having a quiet dinner at the Harvey Mansion downtown. The Harvey Mansion is an historic colonial home that was refashioned into an elegant restaurant. It sits by the Trent River, so George and Linda were both silently admiring the winter sunset through a second-story window by where they were seated.

When the sky's bright pinks and oranges faded to indigo, George said "My daughter called me last night. She and Jake are planning to spend some time with me during Christmas."

"That's nice!" Linda replied, smiling. "It's been a while since you've seen them, hasn't it?"

George said, "Almost a year for Jake. Liz visited me this summer, before I met you. She was having problems with her marriage at the time. Last night she informed she's getting a divorce. She's taking it pretty tough. Jake's got a couple of weeks leave and he's planning on spending most of it with her, so they'll both be coming together. They said they're looking forward to meeting you and Amy, after they got over the initial shock of learning about you." He chuckled at that.

Great communication thought Linda. And she wasn't sure how she felt about it. "So, they didn't know until last night that you were dating someone?" she asked. "Are they okay with it?" *They're both adults who live in other cities, so who cares?*

"Yeah, they're fine with it." and that's all he offered.

"Good. Will they be here Christmas Day? I'm planning a big turkey dinner at my house with my parents coming over, and hopefully you. I'd love to have Liz and Jake join us as well." The last part was a lie. Her house was too small and she didn't know them at all.

"Naw, Babe. I think they'll be here a couple of days the week of Christmas, but they'll be heading out before Christmas Eve. Probably spend some time with their mother while they're here too. I thought I'd take you and Amy out to dinner with us while they're here." *He's so casual about mentioning his ex-wife actually lives here!* That was pretty much all Linda heard. He continued, "I think Amy's going to like Liz. She's real sweet with kids." *He sounds like he thinks Amy's a small child.* Linda was getting a little uncomfortable with her feelings about George, although she knew it didn't make sense. He's been very nice and easy-going, but they've really only known each other a few months now. *To be sure, there's a lot I still don't know about him. Just breathe.*

Linda smiled. "I'm looking forward to meeting them." Then changing the subject, "I had to go to the building inspections office yesterday morning. That Niki woman I told you about has really changed. She was nice! And I think she was being genuine. She mentioned that she would like to have lunch with me some time after the hustle and bustle of the holidays is over. I must say, I'm not used to it. I really think it has something to do with her being over at my neighbor's that day."

"Come on..." George started.

"No, really! I know it sounds absurd, but I really believe it. So does Karen." Linda had a look on her face like little kids get when they're being told a ghost story. George couldn't help but be amused.

"Alright, Babydoll. Maybe there's something to it." he said. "If so, then that's good. But I still want you to keep your guard up when it comes to them – your neighbors I mean."

"Oh, don't you worry about that." Linda assured him. She wished her neighbors would just disappear. She had become weary of the mystery next door.

31

Meanwhile at home, Amy was peering out the window watching. The old car pulled up next door. From the street light, it looked like the old long-haired woman was driving and the big boy Kevin was sitting on the passenger side. His head was down. They just sat out there in the car for a long while. Finally, the dad came out from the house and walked over to them. He didn't gesture much, but Amy could tell he and the woman were having a conversation. Kevin just sat slumped. After another long while, the boy reluctantly got out of the car. He had a big gym bag with him and he followed his dad into the house. The old woman stayed parked in the street for probably five minutes before finally driving off. Amy then proceeded to write her mother a note, then she called her grandparents.

"Can you come and get me? Mom's out with George and I want to spend the night with you. I left Mom a note." Amy said over the phone to her grandma.

"Of course we can, Sweetie." her grandmother answered in her reassuring voice. "Grampa will be there in a few minutes. Have you eaten yet? I made some pizza."

"Yum! I had a little something, but I always have room for your pizza. Thanks!" Amy hung up the phone with relief and packed a small bag.

Amy's note read: *That creepy boy next door came home tonight so I called Grandma and Grampa to come get me. I'll call you in the morning. Love, Amy.*

"Damn I'm glad she called my parents." Linda said as she read the note. "I'm going to call over there though, just so I know for sure she's there." She and George had just come in and it was almost eleven-o-clock, but her parents usually stayed up fairly late.

"She's there and she's fine." Linda said when she came back into the living room. "Dad couldn't understand why I would call since she left a note, but I didn't want to get into all that. Hey, you feel like going dancing? The night's still early."

"My punishment for dating a younger woman." George said. "Why not? Let's go have fun."

32

Over at Grandma's house, Amy was helping decorate their Christmas tree. Grampa was playing a rock opera from the sixties on his stereo, something called Tommy. He always had state of the art stereo systems and Grandma and Grampa both loved music of all genres. Being with them was always fun for Amy, even if they did bicker among themselves. They were so much alike, yet so different. Grampa was a retired Marine, very regimented yet not rigid. He had a great sense of humor and had great integrity. Amy could not think of a finer person than her Grampa. Grandma, on the other hand, was a little crude with her language at times, and she had what seemed to be an extra sense. She could perceive things about people that others could not, and she was usually correct in her perceptions. She was much more relaxed in her character. But she, like Grampa, had a great sense of humor, and that's how they managed to stay together all these years – not to mention she was drop-dead gorgeous in her youth and still was as an older woman.

Linda nor Amy had told either of them about their neighbor's, until this night; Amy felt compelled to tell her grandparents all about the Yard People. However, when she was saying it out loud, she realized how outrageous she sounded.

"Maybe I've told you too many old ghost stories in your little lifetime." Grandma said to Amy. Grampa cut Grandma a look, he wasn't very comfortable with 'ghost stories' – as he was also a religious man. But his wife and daughter were convinced their stories really happened. Amy lit up at the mention of them.

"I love the one about the guitar!" she exclaimed. "Tell me that one, Grandma."

Grandma looked over at Grampa with a smug smile. "Well," she went on, "we were living up north at the time, in an old house we bought from a widow. Your mother was only a few years older than you are now. I had been picking away at the guitar occasionally for many years, probably since your mom was about five years old. I never got any good at it though. Anyway, one day after your mom came home from school, she said to me, 'Mom, I heard you playing the guitar after I went to bed last night. It sounded really beautiful.' Linda, I said, I haven't picked up that old guitar in over a year. I'm not even sure where it is. 'But I was listening to you play before I drifted off to sleep.' your mom said. So, I suggested we look for the guitar. We began searching the house, and do you know where we found it?"

"It was in my mom's closet!" Amy answered excitedly.

"Yes, it was. It was in there behind some boxes and shoes and things." Grandma said. "I have to tell you it really gave us a weird feeling. I wish we could've learned if the widow's husband played guitar."

"That is so cool." Amy got quiet for a few moments after that. She was reflecting on how mysterious and wonderful her grandma is. There was definitely something *special* about her.

Grampa broke the silence when he said, "The tree is starting to shape up. Amy, why don't you put some more red balls throughout it. It needs a just little pop of color."

Amy giggled, "Grampa you should've gone into interior design. You sound like those guys on one of those design shows."

33

The next few days were pretty ordinary. Linda and Amy were getting ready for George to pick them up to have dinner with him and his 'offspring', as Amy liked to say. Linda was thinking about how the holidays are busy enough, *Am I feeling stressed?* without having to have dinner with complete strangers that she'll probably never see again, and still have to act nice. *I think I'm stressing - and I usually love Christmastime.*

They were just about ready when they heard some singing outside. *Carolers?!* She and Amy rushed to the front door and opened it.

"Oh my God!" Linda whispered excitedly under her breath. The small group of carolers was in her front yard about three feet back from the porch steps. "Amy, that's Niki from building inspections and, I suppose, the others are her family." she was saying to Amy while smiling and trying to not move her lips. "I can't believe they're caroling here at our house." Linda didn't really know the ritual for carolers. Was she supposed to offer them a warm drink? Was she supposed to give them money? But since George was due at any moment, she and Amy just stood there smiling, and when their song ended, Linda just smiled, nodded and closed the door before they could begin another.

What Linda and Amy didn't see was when Niki and the other carolers left their house, they went next door and gathered around the front stoop of the Yard People's house. Niki, although she didn't know Linda's neighbors, had come to think of them in a religious sort of way. Like whomever lived there had been touched by God in some way because she felt so uplifted and free ever since her strange visit there. The fact that she couldn't remember anything of that visit only reinforced her new convictions. Now she wanted to get her family and friends in on this wonderful, holy experience. Once they were there however, they just stood quietly for a few moments, then without a word or song, walked off because they all felt disconnected somehow, including Niki. She didn't even know, at this point, why she and her group had come out here.

Linda was relieved to see that Liz and Jake were not with George when he arrived. They were going to meet them at the restaurant, so Linda and Amy started giving George an earful about Niki, and how different she is now, and the Yard People, and so on. George was starting to look uncomfortable, so Linda instructed Amy to not mention anything about the Yard People in front of his kids.

"Don't worry about me, Mom. I don't want to come off as a lunatic." Linda kissed Amy on top of her head.

Liz and Jake were already seated when they arrived at the restaurant. Liz was an attractive brunette with thick sultry lips, the kind actresses pay for, and Jake was very relaxed looking for a military man. He looked very comfortable in his baggy civilian clothing, *he dresses like a rapper,* thought Linda, and he was not real friendly looking. Liz greeted them with a big smile and hugs for everyone while Jake just sat there. *Maybe he had to join the Army because of an attitude problem, but it's not working.*

All throughout the dinner Liz talked on and on about her life. She wasn't complaining, she just liked to talk, a lot. It seemed too that she was purposely avoiding the subject of her marriage. Perhaps it was too painful. Jake, on the other hand, was quiet and spent most of the evening either looking bored to death or, according to Linda, looking at Amy in an inappropriate manner. Neither of them mentioned their mother, and Linda wondered if it was them being polite, or if George had instructed them not to. Or maybe the breakup was really that bad? Thank goodness Liz's conversation was entertaining, she really was an enjoyable girl. She didn't talk so much you felt you were a 'captive' audience. Liz tried to include Amy into the conversation a lot of the time. It was like Liz and Jake were raised by two different families. It's strange how sometimes siblings can be so different from one another. *Maybe it's good I only had Amy; probably dodged a bullet.*

When George dropped Linda and Amy off at their house, there was no activity next door. Linda slightly jumped at the sight of her 'watch dog', which cracked up Amy and George. George gave Linda a light kiss on the cheek, tousled Amy's hair, said good night, and then left.

Linda and Amy sat in the kitchen drinking some decaf coffee and just talking for a while. They didn't talk much about the dinner, there wasn't much to say about it other than they both liked Liz and they both were not impressed with Jake. They mostly talked about school, work, a boy Amy 'sort of'' has a crush on, and things like that. They enjoyed each other's' company - something Linda was grateful for and hoped would never stop. Amy wanted to sleep with her mom that night, and that was just fine with Linda.

34

Christmas morning had arrived. It was a beautiful sunny, crisp morning. Linda was in the kitchen trying to get those aggravating wires from around the slimy, raw turkey's ankles. She kept losing her grip on ol' Tom Turkey and he was banging around in the sink. *Why do they bind your feet anyway? It's not like you're going to go hiking around the goddamn freezer section hunting for corn!* She was still struggling with it when Amy came yawning into the kitchen.

"Hey Baby. Merry Christmas!" Linda said with a big smile on her face, pliers in hand.

"Mele Kaliki Maka Mom." Amy replied, rubbing her eyes. She loved to say it in Hawaiian, only because she knew how. "You need some help there?"

"Yeah, maybe if you could hold him still so I can pry these damn clamps off his feet."

"Why can't you cook him with them on?"

Linda laughed. "Because next I have to spread-eagle him and dig out his innards. Doesn't that sound fun?"

"That's disgusting. Here, let me help you. What time's Grandma and Grampa getting here?" Amy had Tom Turkey wedged in the corner of the sink and was bracing herself with a good foothold against the refrigerator.

"I think they'll get here around noon." Linda replied. "That'll give ol' Tom here about four hours to roast, if I get him started on time, then we can do Christmas presents after dinner. And I'm not expecting George 'til after dinner, he may be here for the gift-giving. Are you excited?"

"Oh, hell yeah!" Amy said, knowing her mom wouldn't get mad about the hell word – it was Christmas after all, and she was helping.

Less than two hours later, the house was filling up with the warm, inviting aroma of roasting turkey and cranberry-scented potpourri simmering. Christmas music was playing and Linda and Amy were all showered and feeling wonderfully anxious. They got started on the rest of the 'fixings' for Christmas dinner. They were having a wonderful time in the kitchen together. Grandma and Grampa drove up after another two hours, right about noon. Amy had forewarned them about the fake watch dog. Grampa came into the house with a bundle of wrapped presents. "Grandma's getting some food out the back seat." he said. "Wow, it smells good in here!"

Linda went out to help her mother and stopped fast on the front porch. Her mother had a tray of cookies in her arms, but she was venturing over into the neighbor's yard. "Mom! What are you doing?" Linda could feel her nerves beginning to unravel. "Mom! Don't!"

Linda's mother looked curiously back at her, then at the neighbor's house. She was standing there like she was listening to something foreign and trying to make sense of it.

"Mom." There was desperation in Linda's tone.

Grandma turned back. "Will you come get this pie out of the car, Linda?"

Linda felt sick and relieved at the same time. She walked over to the car and bent down to reach in, but her mother nudged her with her shoulder. Linda looked up at her.

"I know your father is uncomfortable with my ghost stories and my so-called extra sensory whatever," she was saying, "but there's something terribly wrong over there." She gestured her head toward the neighbor's house. "Amy tried to tell us, but I'm afraid we didn't really taker her seriously. I need to apologize to her."

The Yard People. Linda had never mentioned them to her parents, she didn't want to worry them, and didn't want them to think she was losing it. She had no idea until now that Amy had told them. But now, seeing her mom's reaction, she was really scared. "What are you feeling, Mom?"

"I can't put my finger on it. But, and I know this sounds silly, I feel a lot of sadness from there, but mostly it's an evil essence and it's very strong. Honey, do you know them?" Grandma looked worried.

"No. I've only seen them. They seem to be very poor. But let's not do this now, Mom. It's Christmas and it's a beautiful day." Linda looked hard into her mom's eyes, and they understood each other. Linda retrieved the cherry pie and she and her mother went into the house.

"So," Grampa said, "what's with the dog on the porch? And where's Mr. Macho?" Grampa's impression of George from Thanksgiving was that George was slightly overbearing and walked around a little too puffed up.

"George was here last night, Grampa." Amy giggled. "He said he wouldn't intrude on our family today until after dinner. I don't know if that's polite or rude." Everyone laughed at that.

"And the dog is just a novelty" Linda interjected. "to ward off solicitors."

Eventually Linda and her mother went to the kitchen to finish preparing for the meal while Amy played poker with her grandfather and told him her latest jokes and gossip.

35

Meanwhile, George was pacing back and forth in his apartment, feeling clammy from anticipation. And he didn't want to be too late arriving at Linda's. Finally, at about a quarter past two, the doorbell rang. He opened the door, "I was beginning to think you wouldn't come."

"Shut-up, worm." She snapped and then pushed passed him into the apartment. It was Abby, George's ex-wife. Abby was a petite blonde with chiseled features and a sassy, youthful hair style. She had piercing blue eyes and was in great physical shape.

"I thought maybe Liz told you about my..." George started.

"I know all about your candy-ass girlfriend." Abby cut him off. "I understand you've turned into a real 'family man' these days. Now, get over there in your corner." she said as she jerked her black trench coat off and flung it onto the couch. She was wearing a simple black mini skirt and tank top – Abby was not into costumes. With her commanding presence she knew she didn't need them.

Saying no more, George obeyed. He was standing in his designated corner with his head hung down in shame, all the while becoming aroused. George was the type of man that required the occasional 'punishment'. He didn't know why;

he only knew that Abby understood his needs and was all too willing to fulfill them when she could take time away from her own relationship. This was the one thing that kept them tied to each other. In most broken marriages it was the children that kept a couple from completely severing ties. But with George and Abby it was their perversions – it's not easy to start this type of lifestyle with someone new. Especially in a small, quaint southern town.

"Pull your pants down!" she demanded. "And stop looking down! Hold your head up and don't move away from your corner. I'm going to the kitchen to get some things, and I'd better not come back and catch you with your eyes shut."

George's heart was racing as he stood there with his pants around his ankles, sweat was breaking out on his forehead, and his member was pulsating with agonizing anticipation. Abby took her time in the kitchen, loudly rifling through utensils and the junk drawer, as George's anguish was all part of the stimulation. He was having trouble keeping his head up while he was feeling so much shame. After about five minutes she returned to the living room with some rope and a fly swatter. She didn't bother to pull the shades. She knew too well the possibility of an unexpected audience only heightened the strange thrill of humiliation for him. With bated breath, George was trembling and fully erect. Abby paced slowly back and forth in front of him, never taking her eyes off his hardened penis. Suddenly she slapped him hard across the face, then ordered him to get down on his hands and knees. From there they went into their ritual.

Two and a half hours later, as George was dressing, he was wishing that Abby hadn't fallen out of love with him. Abby was pulling on her coat as she looked at him and said softly, "Why don't you let Linda in on what you're all about? Who knows? She might surprise you."

"I don't know how." George replied. "She's somewhat aggressive, but not like you. And I don't think she would be willing to go as far as you without being repulsed."

"Well, you go ahead and live your double life." said Abby. "But don't expect me to be here for you forever. My current relationship is working out just fine, and although it's a turn-on for my guy when I come here to punish you, I'd really rather be home with him. Merry Christmas, George." And Abby was out the door.

The sun was setting as George stepped into the shower. He was trying to get himself back into his manly mode. He had needed a nap after Abby and now was wondering what excuse he should come up with for being so late on Christmas.

36

Christmas day was wonderful. Even George's absence didn't dampen Linda's spirits. The dinner and gift exchange went great, but being with family was what mattered most to Linda and Amy. It was fun.

Grampa was just finishing up his gross story about the young hung-over marine at the mess hall. "This poor grunt had been out all night boozing it up, and it was about five AM now, and he was in the mess hall hugging a huge stainless steel pot of raw eggs while stirring them with a big a with a wooden spatula. His head was resting on his arm that was around the pot. I happened to walk by just when he puked into the eggs. He never flinched, just kept stirring those eggs." Grampa was laughing so hard. Linda just rolled her eyes and chuckled – she'd heard this one many times growing up.

"That's so disgusting!" exclaimed Amy as she was holding her stomach and covering her mouth with her other hand. "Please tell me you made him throw the eggs out!"

"It didn't matter to me." Grampa said. "I'd already had my breakfast."

"Come on, Dad..." Linda was saying when they all heard something on the porch. At that she said, "George must have finally decided to come celebrate with us."

It had been dark outside for about twenty minutes. Suddenly the front door opened and Kevin from next door was charging into the living room, his eyes glazed. All were stunned for a moment, then Amy screamed, scrambling backward into the hallway.

Everything turned chaotic: Linda's parents were demanding to know what the boy wanted; Linda was rushing to Amy; Grampa tried to block the boy; Grampa was getting knocked down by the boy; Grandma was hitting the boy from behind and trying to get to her husband; the boy was making a b-line for Amy; a lamp got knocked off a table and broke; Grandma was panicking over a cut on Grampa's head and how much it was bleeding; Linda was unsuccessfully struggling with the boy; the Christmas tree was falling over blocking Linda from her parents; and Amy was frantically looking for the gun in Linda's room.

Just as the mayhem began, George was pulling up and parking in front of the house. As he came up the walk, he noticed the front door wide open, then through the dim lighting he saw the fallen Christmas tree and Linda's dad trying to get up from the floor with his wife trying to help him. George turned straight around and headed for his truck to retrieve his gun. As he was coming back up the porch steps, gun cocked and ready, he felt a massive blow to the base of his skull. His last memory would be the sound of his gun firing as his fingers seized by reflex. Dr. James was standing over him clutching a wooden baseball bat that had a spattering of George's blood on it. He was mumbling, "He'll not kill my boy. Not my only boy that might still have a chance."

The earsplitting shot of George's forty-five rang through the house. Linda thought she would lose her mind as she was so desperately trying to pry Kevin away from Amy. He was like a machine that couldn't be stopped. Somehow in the mayhem saw where Amy had dropped their gun! As she picked it up and aimed it at Kevin, Dr. James came charging into the living room.

"No!" shouted Dr. James, as he was flailing the bat in the air and trying to navigate around the fallen Christmas tree. "He doesn't know what he's doing! Don't shoot my boy!"

Kevin had reached Amy and was ripping at her clothes; he had her head and arms pinned with one large arm as he was clawing at her with his other. Amy's struggle was waning because she couldn't catch her breath from his weight on her. Linda could see Amy was close to passing out and the boy wasn't stopping! She looked at Dr. James with a horrified, pleading look, then she aimed the gun, point-blank, at Kevin's knee and fired. Kevin let out a shrilling scream and Dr. James dropped his bat on the floor.

No one could hear the bat drop and roll over the hardwood floor as they were all momentarily deafened by the second gun shot that night. Linda was on the floor holding her daughter in her arms, rocking. Dr. James was helping the stunned, injured boy out of the house. As they limped past Linda's parents, Dr. James paused and said with his head down, "I should've stopped this before now. I'm weak and I'm cursed." As his voice choked, he said, "I'm stopping it now." He and his son left the house.

As the boy and father were stumbling over George's body on the front walk, Linda's mother was dialing 911. She requested an ambulance for her husband and for Amy. She said the neighbors might need one as well. No one in the house knew George had arrived and was now dead. They were all too confused and terrified to even consider where the first shot had come from.

37

Dr. James knew first responders would be coming. He laid Kevin down, who was now unconscious from the trauma, onto Linda's lawn. He slowly turned around and went back to George's body. Tears were rolling down his face as he pulled the gun from George's clenched hand. "I'm stopping it now." he repeated to himself as he entered his home. He knew he didn't have much time. Mark could, and probably would use his mental powers on him now that Kevin was of no use to him.

He went into Mark's room. "How sadly deranged you have become, my son. It's all my fault. I am so sorry." Mark's eyes rolled around toward his dad. He couldn't keep them there for long, they would drift back to the ceiling and then struggle back to his dad. He was still somewhat in a shock from the gunshot – he felt Kevin's pain and fear. What a sickening climax to what was to have been such carnal pleasure!

Dr. James could see the hatred in Mark's eyes. He raised the gun but his arm caught. Mark was forcing *him!* Dr. James's arm was bending at the elbow and his wrist turned – he could not fight it. The gun was pointing at his own head. He stood there like that, with his arm shaking in a spasm, waiting for the gun to go off. It felt like an eternity.

Then his arm slowly began to relax somewhat. Mark had released his hold. Mark's eyes were closed now and he looked peaceful. Then Dr. James felt something come *into* him. It was Mark! For the first time since the accident ten years ago, Mark was communicating with him. *"You're a waste of humanity, old man. Don't expect me to forgive you."* Mark's breathing was labored, *"But I'm ready now. I'm ready for my pitiful, nasty existence to end. Do what you came to do. Do it now!"*

Dr. James was almost in shock. "My son!" he gasped.

"Do it!" Mark opened his eyes again and rolled them around to his dad. Then with an intensity in his eyes, the likes of which Dr. James had never seen ever before, Mark conveyed, *"Do it for Kevin."*

Dr. James didn't notice the sound of the sirens nearing. He moved closer to Mark and raised the gun once more. From less than ten inches to his son's head, he fired. He didn't hear the shot this time, because the sparks from the chamber of the forty-five caused Mark's oxygen tank to explode.

38

It was Christmas night in the quaint little neighborhood in beautiful New Bern. Christmas trees were gleaming, soft lights were glowing, families were gathered, some were still celebrating while others were settling in and reflecting. A house was a-blaze, sirens were sounding, and people were dead.

Linda and her parents were just discovering George's body outside when the explosion went off. The police arrived to find the very unsettling scene. Aside from the house in flames, there was the injured boy laid out in the yard, a dead body on the front walk, a woman in hysterics on the porch with an older couple trying to comfort her, and young dazed girl with a heavy blanket wrapped around her.

39

Christmas day, one year later

"His children blame me, you know." Linda said to Karen as they stood over George's grave in the cemetery. Karen put an arm around Linda's shoulders. It was a cold, gray afternoon and the steam from Linda's breath made her words seem like they were someone else's. It was as though she could still see the words in the air after they were spoken, and they weren't hers. *If only.* "Amy sees that boy Kevin at school sometimes." Linda said as she placed the flowers on George's grave. "He doesn't seem to remember her, or any of that night as far as we know. She says he acts normal, although he's a lot older than the other kids in his grade."

"Well, that's good I believe." said Karen. "Do they talk to each other?"

"Oh, no." Linda turned to look at Karen, her eyes brimming with tears. "Amy just observes him, out of curiosity. Apparently, he went through years of what Amy and Megan experienced, you know, that amnesia episode." Linda and Karen started walking slowly to Karen's SUV. "He lives with his grandmother now, and seems to be doing well. Last week I ran into one of the policemen who came that night, he's a detective now. He told me that the old man was once a doctor or surgeon! And that Kevin's grandmother swears everything that happened last Christmas was caused by the older brother, who was bedridden. We never even knew about an older brother!"

"That's kind of bazaar, though, isn't it?" said Karen. "Blaming someone who's bedridden?"

"I don't know. I always felt like there was something strange and creepy about the Yard People." Linda stopped in her tracks. "I guess the grandmother knows what she's talking about. After all, she and the others never would go into the house. They always stayed in their vehicles, so the dad & son only talked to them from the yard."

About the Author

Diana Bottone is from Wilmington, NC and currently resides in New Bern, NC. She is a mother, a grandmother, and a retired State worker who loves to play golf, travel, and play trivia with friends. She also dabbles in painting and poetry, and volunteers with various local organizations.

The daughter of a Marine, Diana has lived in many places. She has called New Bern her home since 1980.